ANGEL AND THE ACTRESS

An enthralling crime mystery full of twists

ROGER SILVERWOOD

Yorkshire Murder Mysteries Book 23

JOFFE BOOKS

Revised edition 2021
Joffe Books, London
www.joffebooks.com

First published in Great Britain in 2015
as *Angel and the Actress*

ISBN: 978-1-78931-696-4

ONE

The Mansion House, Ceresford Road, Bromersley, South Yorkshire
Sunday, 2 November 2014, 9 p.m.

Seventy-six-year-old Joan Minter was standing on the shiny black grand piano in stockinged feet. She was wearing a two thousand-pound-dress and was meticulously made up except, perhaps, for the carmine painted over the natural outline of her lips. She was holding a glass of champagne in one hand and a cigarette in the other. The glass and the cigarette shook precariously as she addressed the small show-business gathering. She spoke loudly as if she was making her curtain speech to the back row of the gods.

'Friends,' she began, 'friends, I have invited you here this evening to join me in a very special celebration.' Then with a mischievous twinkle, she said, 'I had invited David, Errol, Rodney and Michel, but surprisingly, none of them were able to come . . .'

They were the names of her four ex-husbands from whom she had had the most acrimonious divorces and enjoyed a great deal of valuable publicity. The gathering appreciated the joke, smiled and several people laughed out loud.

Still smiling, she continued, 'None of them were able to make it. Today is *not* the date I married or divorced any of them. Well, I don't think it is. I can't remember. *Nor* is it my fortieth birthday.'

Several smiled.

'No, that's next year, Joan, isn't it?' one of the guests called out.

She smiled back at him, then changed the mood by taking a breath, holding it, biting her lip, turning her head slowly through ninety degrees and waiting. The room was silent.

'I asked you all to come to this special celebration,' she said with a catch in her voice and a hand to her chest, 'because it is seventy years since I first entered show business. It is seventy years to this very day since my dear mamma took me on the train to the Empire Theatre, Sheffield, to audition before the great Cedric Masters to become one of his Marigold girls and be in his pantomime, *Cinderella*, that winter.'

'Hurrah for Joan,' an actor, Felix Lubrecki, called out. 'Let's drink to that.'

The guests raised their glasses. 'To Joan and the last seventy years,' they said in unison.

Another actor, Leo Altman, raised his glass. 'And here's to the *next* seventy years,' he said.

Joan smiled and put the cigarette to her mouth.

Then, suddenly, the lights went out. The room went black. There was a loud bang, the flash from a gun from amid the guests, followed by a gasp and a thud from the direction of the piano.

'Oh my God!' several people said. 'What's happened?'

'Put the lights on,' a voice said.

'Where is the switch?' said another.

There was a sound from the entrance hall of the front door being slammed.

The door into the room from the kitchen opened. A stream of light shone through onto the carpet and the two staff from the outside caterers — a man and a woman — rushed in to find out what the disturbance was.

The light made it possible to see around the drawing room, and the butler, who had been standing by the piano, rushed across the room to the light-switch panel by the door from the hall and switched on the room lights.

There were gasps from some of the people there as they saw the body of Joan Minter on the carpet by the piano, blood running from her head over her thin, silver-grey hair.

The butler rushed across to her, crouched down, leaned over and touched her neck with his fingertips.

'Is there a pulse?' Felix Lubrecki said.

After a few seconds the butler slowly shook his head.

Forty-five minutes later, Detective Inspector Michael Angel drove a BMW up the drive to the Mansion House and parked behind a white Scene-of-Crime Officers' van, which was itself behind a police patrol car. As he turned off the lights and the ignition, he saw the lights of a fourth vehicle in his rear mirror. It was stopping close behind him. He got out of the car and discovered that the driver of the car behind was one of his team, Detective Sergeant Flora Carter.

'Oh, it's you, Flora,' he said.

'Good evening, sir,' she said. 'So this is where the famous Joan Minter lives?'

'Apparently,' he said as they walked up in the moonlight towards the constable on the door. 'I don't like turning out of the house at this time on a Sunday night. Mary wasn't best pleased, either.'

Flora Carter smiled. She had met the DI's wife and considered her to be a most delightful lady.

The constable on the front doorstep blew into his hands and stamped his feet. As he recognized DI Angel approaching, he saluted. 'Good evening, sir,' he said.

Angel reciprocated. 'I hope so, Constable. I really do,' he said. 'Has Dr Mac been summoned, do you know, lad? I can't see his car anywhere?'

'Don't know, sir,' the constable said as he opened the front door. 'He's not inside. I'm certain of that. DS Taylor is in there with a couple of his team.'

'Right, Constable, thank you.'

Angel ushered DS Carter into the hall and then followed her in.

The constable closed the door.

A door opened into the hall and a man came in. He was wearing a white overall, white hat, rubber gloves, a linen mask and blue wellingtons.

It was DS Taylor. He was in charge of the SOCO team at Bromersley Police station. 'There you are, sir,' he said, pulling the face mask down.

Angel sighed. 'What's up, Don? I was told that the famous Joan Minter has been shot dead.'

'That's what it looks like, sir,' Taylor said. 'There's no gun, but we've found the shell case of a .32 in the corner of the room by the door. Miss Minter was having a party with some friends. I had to clear them out of there. Looks like two rooms knocked into one. It's a drawing room, really, with a long dining table in the centre where they've had a meal. There isn't another room on this floor that is big enough for everybody to get together. The guests are now in various parts of the house, all whingeing about wanting to go home. One man came up to me and said he would have to leave. He lives in Hollywood.'

Angel's eyebrows shot up. 'Hollywood? Anyone we've heard of?'

'Erick Cartlett, sir. I've never heard of him. It's a heck of a long way to come for a party.'

'Are there any witnesses?'

'They're all witnesses, sir. In the sense that they were all present at the time of the gunshot.'

Angel rubbed his chin. 'Well, we can't keep everybody waiting round forever. Where we can gather them together?'

'Here, I should think, sir. This hall,' Taylor said.

Angel turned to DS Carter. 'Whip round the house, Flora, and ask everybody to assemble here immediately.'

'Right, sir,' she said, and she dashed off up the stairs.

Angel said, 'Did you hear from Dr Mac, Don? I want him to see the body as soon as possible.'

'Duty sergeant told me he'd been advised.'

'Good. Have you much more to do in there?'

Taylor said, 'About twenty minutes, sir. We should be through.'

'I'll have to chase Mac up. I want him to see the body in situ.'

There was the sound of several voices on the landing above them. Angel broke away from Taylor and looked up the staircase.

'I'll get back to my boys, sir,' Taylor said.

'Right, Don,' Angel said.

Taylor turned and made off towards the door.

Angel called up the stairs. 'Come down here, please, everybody.'

Ten minutes later, the guests and staff were assembled in the hall. Angel introduced himself, said how sorry he was that he had to investigate the death of their dear friend, pointed out that sadly it had to be done and asked for their patience and cooperation. Then he said, 'Firstly, looking around you, is anybody missing that was in the house at the time Miss Minter was delivering her speech?'

A tubby man in a dress suit and tails stepped forward and said, 'I am . . . I was Miss Minter's butler, sir, and I can tell you that there are ten guests, two persons from the caterers, and myself. If you would care to count us, it might be quicker.'

Angel thanked him, turned to Flora, jerked his head and she began the count.

He then turned back to the butler. 'What is your name?'

'Alexander Trott, sir.'

'Mr Trott, do you happen to have a list of the guests?'

'Indeed I do, sir,' he said, reaching into his inside pocket. 'I also have their addresses and telephone numbers.'

Angel smiled.

Trott passed him a printed list of all the guests.

'Thank you,' Angel said. He glanced at it, then looked up and said, 'Did anybody see anything suspicious?'

There was silence.

DS Carter came back to Angel and quietly said, 'Thirteen, sir, not counting you and me.'

Angel nodded. The count was correct. 'Thank you, Flora.'

'Did anybody see anyone with a gun?'

There were a few murmurs of 'No'.

'Was anybody standing close to the person with the gun?'

A young man stepped forward. 'I was only about six feet away from the flash of the gun when it was fired.'

'Thank you, sir. What is your name?'

'My name is Felix Lubrecki,' he said. 'I worked with Joan many times. I played her halfwit son in a film called *Beware My Vision*. I shall miss her terribly.'

'I'm sorry,' Angel said. 'Did you not have a sense of the person with the gun? His or her height? Male or female? Smell of anything? Alcohol, mint or perfume? How they were dressed; light frilly dress or stiff black dinner jacket?'

'I'm sorry, I couldn't say, Inspector. It happened so suddenly and unexpectedly. The flash was blinding.'

'And where were you standing exactly?'

'About six feet away, by the door to the hall.'

Angel's forehead creased. 'Did anybody else see the flash of the gun? Did it illuminate the person holding it?'

A man about sixty years of age said, 'Yeah. I saw the flash. It didn't illuminate anything. It was a bright yellow and white light lasting only a split second. It only blinded you, momentarily; it did not illuminate anything.'

Angel said, 'Where were you standing at the time you saw this, sir? And what is your name?'

'Leo Altman. I have been a friend of Joan for many years . . . I was standing just behind Felix.'

'Thank you, Mr Altman. And how near were you to the door?'

'Only a couple of feet, I suppose.'

'You would know when the door opened and when it closed, wouldn't you?'

'Erm . . . I was listening to Joan,' Altman said. 'She was very funny . . . I can't be sure about the door *before* the lights went out. I believe that somebody went out *after* the gunshot. The sound of the gun deafened me for a few seconds.'

'Was the door to the hall ajar at the time of the gunshot?' Angel said.

Lubrecki looked round the other guests. No one seemed inclined to answer. He said, 'It was closed, Inspector, I think. Because it must have been opened shortly afterwards otherwise we would not have heard the front door close.'

'Thank you, Mr Lubrecki,' Angel said, then he pursed his lips. 'Did anybody else hear the front door close shortly after the gunshot?'

Several guests said, 'Yes.'

'And when the door to the hall was opened did it not shine a light into the drawing room?'

'No,' a few small voices said.

Angel said, 'Does everybody agree that the hall light must therefore also have been switched off?'

'Yes,' many more said confidently.

'Anybody disagree?'

Almost everybody looked around, but nobody took the opposite view.

'Is it reasonable, then, to assume that the hall was also in total darkness?'

Again, nobody answered.

Angel breathed out loudly and rubbed his chin. He wasn't pleased.

The butler, Alexander Trott, was the nearest to the inspector. Angel eyed him. Trott thought that he was consequently being called upon to answer.

'Yes, sir,' Trott said, 'although I was standing near the piano, I heard the drawing-room door being opened immediately after the gunshot and before the front door was heard to close. And no light shone into the drawing room from the hall.'

'Thank you, Mr Trott,' Angel said.

Then addressing everybody, Angel said, 'Has anybody any idea *why* Miss Minter was murdered?'

'No,' several voices said.

An elderly man stepped forward. He spoke with an Atlantic accent. 'I'm Erick Cartlett, everybody here knows me,' he said.

Angel thought the name was familiar, not as an actor, but he thought he had seen his name appear in the credits at the beginning of TV films . . . as a producer or as a writer who was also a director. He wasn't sure.

'Isn't it perfectly obvious,' Cartlett said, 'that the murderer was a stranger who sneaked into the house and entered the drawing room while Joan had our full attention? He then switched off the lights, fired the gun, then ran out of the room across the hall and out of the front door.'

There were plenty of nods and grunts of agreement with what Cartlett had said.

Angel ran his tongue round his mouth and said, 'That's a possibility, Mr Cartlett, but only a possibility. I can't take anything for granted.'

'It seems a darn right certainty, if you ask me,' he said. 'And by the by I have to be at a very important meeting in Beverley Hills on Tuesday, so I hope you will not delay me and cause me to miss it.'

Angel said, 'We will do our best, Mr Cartlett.'

A woman with wet cheeks, red eyes and a face puffy from crying came forward. She had a small voice and was given to a lot of rapid blinking. 'If you disagree with Mr Cartlett's theory, Inspector,' she said, 'it means that the person with the gun is . . . is one of us, and it is possible that he or she is here . . . here with us, in this room, now.'

'I'm afraid that that is so,' Angel said. 'May I have your name, miss?'

'Jane Bell,' she said. 'I'm Miss Minter's secretary — well, I was. I don't know what I shall do now.' She turned away, digging in her pocket for a tissue.

'I am so sorry,' Angel said.

Jane Bell applied the tissue to her face, turned away with a gentle wave and got lost among the guests.

Angel sighed. He thought a moment then looked at his watch. It was 10.30. Then he looked up and said, 'Perhaps you would wish to retire for the night and we will continue our enquiries in the morning. Would everybody please remain accessible, and not leave the house until this matter is satisfactorily concluded? Thank you.'

There was some discontented muttering, but most of the guests were pleased to retire to their rooms and they all shuffled slowly up the stairs.

Angel turned to DS Carter. 'I'll have to see the caterers. Where are they?'

'They were here a moment ago. I expect they've gone into the kitchen.'

Angel and DS Carter went through the door from the hall to the kitchen and saw one of the caterers had removed his jacket and hung it on a coat hanger on the back of the door. He was wearing a big blue and white striped apron, and was busy drying pots from the draining board and putting them onto the table. The woman was standing at the sink. She had a bowl full of pots and was washing them and putting them on the draining board.

The caterers glanced across at Angel and Carter and then turned away.

Angel said, 'If you'll excuse me, I am Detective Inspector Angel and this is Detective Sergeant Carter. There are a few questions I need to ask.'

The man didn't look pleased. He sniffed and said, 'We want to go to bed, sir. It's gone half past ten. We're expected to be back in here, bright and chirpy in the morning, from seven o'clock to serve ten breakfasts. If we don't get these done tonight we shall not be able to, so what is it you want and would you keep it short?'

Angel's face reddened. His fists tightened. 'I am investigating a murder, sir. A *real* murder. Not playing a parlour game. Bringing a murderer to justice is far more important than your ten breakfasts. I need your full attention and I am afraid it will take . . . just as long as it has to take.'

The woman took her hands out of the sink, removed her rubber gloves and turned to face Angel.

The man, seeing she had given in, sighed, banged the plate he had been wiping down on the table, threw the cloth on top of it, looked wearily at Angel and said, 'Right. What do you want to know?'

Angel stared back at him. 'Thank you,' he said. 'Well, for a start, what's your name?'

'Robert Jones,' the man snapped.

Angel's lips tightened back against his teeth. 'Mr Jones,' he said, 'we are also tired, but we won't finish here for another hour or two, so you are not on your own.'

Jones sighed, folded his arms across his chest, pursed his lips and blew out a silent whistle.

Angel said, 'Where were you when the shooting took place?'

'In here. Cleaning pans and washing up.'

'Then what did you do?'

'At the time we didn't do anything. Well, we carried on with what we were doing. We heard the shot, of course, but these people are all in the entertainment business; we didn't know at first if it was part of a play or the bursting of a balloon or some other nonsense. It was nothing to do with us. We're here to feed them, that's all. A few minutes after that, I realized that they had stopped laughing. So I opened the kitchen door a little and looked in. Guests were crowded round the carpet near the piano. It dawned on me that there must be something up.'

Angel turned to the young lady. 'And what is your name, miss?'

She smiled. 'Charlotte Jones,' she said. 'He's my husband.' She moved towards him, then she and Robert exchanged smiles.

Angel smiled at her. 'Ah, yes, Mrs Jones. I see. And what did you do when you heard the gunshot?'

'As Robert said, sir. We didn't take much notice at first.'

Angel said, 'Did you hear the front door close?'

Jones said, 'Yes. Just after the gunshot.'

'Did the lights in here go out when the murderer switched the drawing-room lights off?'

'No. They can only be switched on and off in here,' Jones said. He pointed to the switch in a brass panel on the wall by the door to the hall. 'There's a two-way switch there.' Then he pointed to the door into the drawing room. 'And another there.'

Angel screwed up his face, looked at Carter and said, 'Have you got that, Flora?'

She looked up from her notebook. 'Yes, sir.'

Angel traversed the kitchen and tried each switch in turn. It was just as Jones had said. 'Thank you,' he said. 'That's all for tonight. I'm sorry to have held you back.'

He turned away from them and made for the door.

Robert Jones thoughtfully picked up the kitchen cloth and a plate off the draining board and began to wipe it. Charlotte noticed and, taking her cue from him, looked round for the rubber gloves to resume washing the pots.

As Angel reached the door he turned to Carter and said, 'Flora, be sure to get their address and phone number. I'm going to see if I can find Don Taylor.'

He went into the hall and closed the kitchen door.

He then went next door to the drawing room. He opened the door and looked in. The three SOCO men, all dressed in white, were in a huddle by the piano. A fourth was on his knees on the floor. They all turned to face him.

'Are you ready, Don?' Angel said.

'Yes, sir,' Taylor said. 'Near enough.'

Angel went in and before he touched the door handle on the inside said, 'I've no gloves, Don.'

'It's all right, sir. What was on there was smudged out of all recognition.'

Angel closed the door.

The man on his knees was Dr Mac the pathologist, an old friend of Angel's.

The doctor stood up, moved to one side to put something in his bag and revealed to Angel the crumpled body of Joan Minter on the cream carpet close to the piano. Her eyes were open and staring, her face strangely white around pink patches on her cheeks, which had obviously been applied from a pot. The sparse silver-grey hair was covered, on one side, with congealed blood; by her side was a champagne flute and about a metre away from that, a burnt-out cigarette.

It wasn't a pretty sight. But he had seen worse, much worse.

Angel leaned over the body, his eyes scanning the scene, trying to memorize every detail. After a few moments he straightened up, wrinkled his nose, looked at Mac and said, 'Any idea about the gun?'

'I'll tell ye what I can when I get the slug oot,' the elderly Glaswegian medic said in an accent all his own.

'Just the one shot?'

'Aye. That's what it looks like,' Mac said.

Taylor said, 'We think that's it, sir. We've inspected the target area, the piano and the wall behind. No damage.'

Angel nodded.

'And there's only one bullet case over there by the door,' Taylor added.

Angel looked back at the door. He saw a police marker with the letter A painted on it.

He rubbed his chin. 'The murderer must have been very confident, firing just one round in the dark like that,' Angel said. Then he turned to the doctor and said, 'Have you got anything interesting, Mac?'

'It looks straightforward enough,' the doctor said. 'Intruder sneaks into the hoose when everybody's attention is on the host. Switches off light. Fires gun from doorway. Then under cover of darkness makes his or her escape. All that I have so far agrees with that account of what happened.'

Angel nodded.

The door behind them opened. They all turned towards it. It was DS Carter.

'There you are, sir,' she said.

'Come in, Flora,' Angel said.

Taylor said, 'Any point in examining the witnesses for gunshot residue, sir? It might tell us who was the *nearest* to the one who fired the gun.'

Angel jerked his head back in surprise. 'Yes, of course. It might even tell us the one who actually *fired* the gun,' he said. 'Flora will give you a hand.'

She looked at him and nodded.

'In fact, Don,' Angel said, 'if you get a really positive result from any of the witnesses, I shall want you to carry out a paraffin wax test.'

Taylor nodded.

'And better check out that cigarette she was smoking . . . and the contents of that champagne flute. You never know.'

'Right, sir,' Taylor said.

'I'll have the body moved now, if it's all right with you, Michael,' Mac said.

Angel nodded and turned away to Carter as the doctor tapped a number into his mobile.

Angel said, 'Flora, at first light tomorrow, I'll need you to instigate a search for the weapon. You'll want a dozen men or more.'

Flora Carter's eyes grew very big. 'Have you seen the size of the grounds, sir? It's like Epping Forest.'

'Yes, well, confine it to the house and, say, ten metres from the outside walls for a start. If we don't find it, we may have to think again.'

'Right, sir.'

'And will you ring the nick and liaise with the duty sergeant for two uniformed officers to cover this house for the next thirty-six hours at least? Then you'd better push off and get some rest. Meet me here at seven o'clock tomorrow morning.'

She smiled. 'Right, sir,' she said.

'On your way out, will you find that butler chap, Trott? I don't know where he'll be. Tell him . . . *ask* him to call in and see me. I'll be here for another few minutes or more.'

'Righto, sir,' she said. 'Goodnight.'

'Aye. What's left of it.'

She left the room and closed the door.

Taylor came up to him having taken off his whites and was carrying them under his arm. 'Goodnight, sir. Goodnight, Doctor. See you in the morning.'

'Goodnight, Don.'

'Goodnight, Don. If you see the men from the mortuary looking lost, point them in here, will you?'

'Will do,' he said. He went out and closed the door.

Mac was still pulling off his whites. He looked at Angel and, with a twinkle in his eye, said, 'I might have known this would be *your* case, Michael. You always get a very low standard of murderer. Those who have no regard at all for my delicate Presbyterian upbringing. None of them seem to work a respectable nine-to-five day for five days a week, with Saturdays and Sundays free.'

Angel smiled. 'Come off it, Mac. I bet you weren't doing anything important.'

'How do you know what I was doing?'

Angel grinned. 'I know you. You'd be either sewing up a hole in your kilt, preparing some porridge for the morning, warming up some haggis for your supper, re-cataloguing your thistle collection or converting your bagpipes to metric. You're a real credit to the SNP.'

Mac shook his head. He couldn't avoid a little smile. 'Your imagination knows no bounds.'

There was a knock at the door.

'Come in,' Angel said.

It was the butler. 'You wanted me, sir?'

'Ah yes, Mr Trott. Thank you for coming. Is there a small room that I could use for a couple of days or so that would be suitable as an interview room?'

He frowned momentarily, then said, 'There's the small sitting room off the hall, sir. It would seat about four persons. Madam used to use it whenever she wanted to watch television.'

'Thank you, Mr Trott. Sounds ideal.'

'I'll see it's ready for you tomorrow.'

'And would you ask everybody to wear the same clothes tomorrow morning that they were wearing this evening?'

Trott frowned again, then waited.

Angel didn't know if he was waiting for a tip or something. Then he thought he must be waiting for an explanation. Angel had no intention of explaining. He didn't want the guests washing or brushing evidence away.

'Thank you, Mr Trott,' Angel said. 'Goodnight to you.'

Trott shook himself out of his questioning look. 'Erm . . . very good, sir. I'll spread the word. Goodnight, sir,' he said, and he went out.

Mac pointed towards the door and said, 'Strange fellow.'

'Just what I was thinking,' Angel said. 'Are you ready for off?'

'I'll just wait for my men from the mortuary.'

'I'll wait with you,' Angel said. He looked at his watch. 'It's five minutes to midnight. I have to check that there will be constables on duty here through the rest of the night. And they change over in five minutes.'

There was another knock at the door.

'Come in,' Angel said.

Two men in peaked caps, one carrying a folded stretcher, looked in.

Mac knew them. 'Come on through, Brendan. The body's by the piano.'

TWO

24 Ceresford Road, Bromersley, South Yorkshire
Monday, 3 November 2014, 10 p.m.

A man walked up the long drive of the architect-designed, five-bedroom house in the more salubrious part of Bromersley. He passed the new blue Ford Mondeo parked outside the front door, hardly giving it a glance. He climbed the two stone steps and pressed the doorbell.

It was eventually answered by a middle-aged woman.

'Mrs Cross?' the young man said.

'No,' she said. 'No. The name is Sellars. Who were you wanting?'

The young man looked at the piece of paper he was holding. He frowned. 'I am looking for Mr Cross, 24 Ceresford Park Road.'

'This is 24 Ceresford Road, all right, but there's no "Park" in the address.'

'Oh?' he said, pointing to the paper. 'It definitely says Ceresford *Park* Road. Is it anywhere round here?'

'Don't know of it,' Mrs Sellars said with a smile. 'There's a Park Road at the end of this road going towards Rotherham. It might be that.'

'Oh yes. Is it? Right. Which way do I go?'

'You go back down our drive, out of the gate and turn left. Go on to the lights, then turn right. That's Park Road.'

He looked puzzled. 'Oh. Right,' he said. 'Thank you.'

Mrs Sellars withdrew into the house and made to close the door.

The young man suddenly said, 'Do you happen to know if a Mr Cross lives there at number 24?'

The woman came out again. 'I've no idea,' she said. 'But you could try there and ask.'

'Yes,' he said. 'Er, right. Er, thank you very much. Erm . . . I notice that you have a very big garden, haven't you?'

Mrs Sellars frowned, then raised her eyebrows and put her hands on her hips. She breathed in deeply, eyed him closely and said, 'What do you really want, young man?'

He avoided her eyes and said, 'I wondered if you were looking for . . . I wondered if you needed a gardener.'

She blinked. 'No. We don't, thank you,' she said. 'We already have help in that regard. Now, if you'll excuse me I have to go.' She withdrew into the house and began to close the door.

'Do you know anybody who does, missis?' he called.

'No. Sorry,' she said and closed the door firmly, turned the key in the lock and leaned back against it. She frowned. She wasn't pleased. She sensed that there was something odd about the man, but she couldn't quite put her finger on it. She walked thoughtfully down the polished parquet hall to the kitchen door and went inside. Maybe he was simply very lonely. There was a lot of loneliness in the world. Or maybe he needed a job. Maybe the man he was looking for — a Mr Cross — was seeking a gardener.

She looked round to see what she had been doing before the disturbance. She saw the coffee percolator on the work-top with its lid off and a new packet of coffee by its side. She had just picked up a kitchen knife to make a hole in the packet when she noticed a cold breeze at the back of her neck. She whipped round to find the back door slightly open. That was strange. She was certain it had been closed. The wind suddenly picked up and blew it wide open.

She crossed the kitchen quickly, grabbed hold of the door handle, then stepped outside and looked around. A cloud of brown, black and red leaves swirled around the doorstep. The wind blew a strand of hair across her face. She moved it back over an ear. Then she noticed the back gate was slightly ajar. It had certainly not been left like that. It never was. It was always closed and the latch down. Then the penny dropped: while her attention had been taken talking to that man at the front door, somebody had been in the kitchen.

She quickly came back into the house, closed the door and turned the key. She looked round the kitchen to see if anything had been taken.

Her handbag had been on the table. It had gone. Her heart missed a beat. Her hand went up to her chest. She suddenly felt as if she had a frozen cannonball in the middle of her stomach. Her handbag had contained about a hundred pounds in cash, her credit cards, her mobile phone, several family photographs and items of no interest to anybody else but of great value to her.

Then she had a thought. She rushed back up the hall to the front door. She unlocked it and opened it to see the rear of her new blue Ford Mondeo disappear up the drive and out into the road.

The car key had been in the handbag.

Her chest tightened. Her breathing accelerated. She promptly turned back into the house, picked up the phone in the hall, dialled 999.

A constable asked a lot of questions about her and about the car, and required a description of the man, which she patiently gave to him in detail. Then he repeated all the information back to her to be sure that he had it all down correctly and that any unusual words were spelled correctly.

She had just put the phone down when it rang out. She snatched it up. It was her husband phoning from his office in the centre of Bromersley, about a mile away. Before she had chance to tell him her news, he said, 'I've been trying to reach you, Vera. My car has just been stolen. One of the girls saw a man simply walk up to it, unlock the door, start the engine and drive it out of my parking space. He must have had a key.'

Her mouth fell open.

The spare key to her husband's silver Volkswagen Jetta had also been in her handbag.

The Mansion House, Bromersley, South Yorkshire
Monday, 3 November 2014, 11 a.m.

Angel was in the small sitting room off the hall. He was seated behind a small antique ormolu table that had been moved to the middle of the room, which was adequately furnished with several chairs, and a big television almost concealed by a fire screen.

He had his notes in front of him and was reading through them when there was a knock at the door.

'Come in,' he called.

It was DS Carter. Her face glowed. Her eyes were dancing. 'We've found the gun, sir.'

Angel's eyebrows went up. 'Where?' he said, standing up. 'Whereabouts?'

'On the lawn, not far from the front door,' she said.

'Show me,' he said.

Carter turned round and made for the door. Angel went round the table and followed her. They went out through the front door, down the steps and onto the drive.

On the lawn beyond, a small crowd of policemen and women in high-visibility coats and carrying long sticks were talking among themselves. They looked round as Angel and the sergeant approached.

Carter led the way on to the grass, and about two metres from the gravel drive, on the closely cut lawn, she pointed downwards. 'There, sir,' she said.

The group of police who had been searching the grounds and the house came in closer.

Angel looked down at the handgun. He recognized the make immediately.

'Ah,' he said, giving a deep and satisfying sigh. 'It's an old Walther, PPK/S .32 automatic.'

He turned to the group and said, 'Who found it?'

'I did, sir,' a young man said with a grin.

'Well done, lad,' Angel said. 'And what's your name?'

'Atkinson, sir,' he said, enjoying the moment and looking round to see if his workmates were noticing him.

'I'll remember that,' Angel said. Then he looked at the others. 'Nobody's touched it, have they?' he added.

A few voices muttered, 'No, sir.'

'Good,' he said, then he looked at the young policeman and said, 'Stay with this gun, Atkinson, and don't let anybody near it until SOCO assume responsibility for it. All right?'

'Right, sir,' Atkinson said, still grinning.

Angel turned to Carter and said, 'Ask Don Taylor to deal with it ASAP. Have you much more to search?'

'No, sir, but I said I'd assist Don with the vacuuming of the witnesses' clothing.'

'Right,' Angel said. 'The women will prefer another woman for that job, obviously. I'll get Crisp to take over from you, but carry on with the searching until he arrives.'

She nodded in agreement and turned away.

Then Angel set off back to the little sitting room, tapping out a number on his mobile as he went. He was phoning his other detective sergeant. He closed the sitting-room door and sat down at the ormolu table. He had the phone to his ear listening to the ringing tone.

To look at, Detective Sergeant Trevor Crisp was straight out of a 1940s Hollywood list of leading men: tall, dark and handsome. He was in his thirties, unmarried and had been seen many times hanging around with WPC Leisha Baverstock, the station beauty. They had been engaged at least twice but where their relationship was at any given time, nobody knew. Crisp wasn't a gifted detective. He wasn't even hard-working. In fact, Angel frequently couldn't find him. But he was very useful in dealing with women witnesses and villains. He could wheedle round a female better than anybody else at Bromersley nick, and he could handle tough, rough recidivists when necessary.

Angel's phone was answered.

'Good morning, sir,' DS Crisp said.

'There you are,' Angel said. 'I want you over here on this Joan Minter murder ASAP. What are you doing?'

'I'm looking into the strange case of the robbery of two cars from the same family, sir.'

'Oh?' Angel said, and began to tug on an ear. 'Were they luxury cars . . . Rolls Royce or Jaguar or . . . ?'

'No, sir. One was a Ford and the other a Volkswagen,' Crisp said. 'They were stolen from different addresses within five minutes of each other. The Ford was almost new and the Volkswagen only two years old. There were two in the gang. I have a witness who saw and spoke to one of them.'

Angel ran the tip of his fingers repeatedly over an eyebrow. 'Looks like some big fish tooling up for a job.'

'That's what I thought.'

'Have you shown the witness our rogues' gallery?'

'She's looking through it now, sir.'

Angel frowned and tapped his fist against his lips. Eventually he said, 'It sounds as if you might be close to a result there.'

'I believe so, sir. Can't be sure, of course. It depends on the witness.'

Angel wrinkled his nose. 'I expect she's a blonde, about thirty,' he said.

Crisp grinned. 'No, sir. She's got mousy-coloured hair and is about fifty. But you're right about being close to a result. I might be able to sew it up if she picks out the villain.'

'Right. Stay where you are, then, for the moment. We'll manage. But let me know how you get on.'

Angel ended the call and pocketed the mobile. He rubbed his chin. He took out the mobile again and tapped in a number. It began to ring out.

At last it was answered. 'CID, DC Ahaz speaking. Can I help you?'

'Ahmed?' Angel said.

'Yes, sir,' the young man answered brightly. 'Good morning, sir.'

'What are you busy with?'

Ahmed smiled. His eyes sparkled. It sounded as if an interesting job might be in the offing. 'Only filing, sir,' he said.

'Come out here then, ASAP. I want you. We're very short-handed. Tell the duty sergeant, and ask him if there's any transport coming this way, otherwise you'll have to walk.'

Ahmed Ahaz's eyes sparkled. 'Right, sir. I won't be long.'

Angel smiled as he ended the call. He could always depend on Ahmed. He was enthusiastic, willing to learn, a hard worker and conscientious. Angel thought he had the makings of a great detective.

He stuffed the mobile into his pocket. He was considering what to do next when there was a knock at the door.

'Come in,' he said.

It was DS Taylor. He was carrying a polythene bag with the word EVIDENCE printed in big red letters across it.

'What is it, Don?' Angel said.

'The Walther,' Taylor said, holding out the bag.

Angel took it and put it on the tabletop.

'As expected there are no prints,' Taylor said. 'I've got Records looking up the serial number. It was brought here fully loaded. I've taken seven bullets out. The eighth was the bullet case, which was found, which is the same bore, and which presumably killed Joan Minter.'

'Better check the firing-pin mark,' Angel said.

He nodded. 'Will do.'

'Any prints on any of them?'

'Polished clean, sir,' he said. Then the muscles round his mouth tightened. He cleared his throat as he added, '*Very* professionally.'

Angel rubbed his hand hard across his mouth. He nodded and said, 'It's all very worrying, Don.'

'I'll get back to my team, sir,' Taylor said, and turned to go.

'Right. Is everything going all right? How far have you got?'

'I've almost finished the male guests, sir. Had a bit of trouble with one of them . . . an American called Erick Cartlett. He said that I'd no right to subject him to that sort of indignity. He prattled on about his human rights and all that. And he wants to see you.'

'I'll see *him* first. Send him along, will you?'

Taylor said, 'Right, sir, I will. And the butler, Trott, did you want me to check him for gunshot residue? I mean, he was only a few feet away from Miss Minter when she was shot.'

'May as well. And the two caterers, as well. Everybody who was there.'

'Right, sir.'

'I expect Mac will vacuum the clothes Joan Minter was wearing?'

Suddenly, without warning, the door opened and a man with thick spectacles, grey hair and a red face burst in. He came up to Angel, pointed a finger at him and in an American drawl said, 'I wanna see you, mister.'

Angel and Taylor stared at him.

'Yes, sir?' Angel said. 'What can I do for you?'

Taylor turned back to Angel and said, 'This is Mr Cartlett, sir. I was telling you about him.'

The American's face grew redder. 'Yes, Erick Cartlett is my name,' he said. 'You may have heard of me.'

Angel had never heard the name so it made no impression on him.

'Please take a seat,' he said. 'Won't keep you a moment.'

Cartlett's lips went a blue colour. In a menacing voice, he said, 'I won't wait long, young man.'

Angel turned to Taylor and said, 'Had we finished, Don? Where were we?'

'I just wanted to ask about Flora, sir. You said that she would be helping me. I haven't got a woman in my team, and a female pair of hands would be—'

'Yes, Don. I know. Women don't like being touched by men they don't know. Flora is coming to you when she's finished the search. I should think she's near the end of it by now. Liaise with her, will you? She's somewhere around the house and grounds. If you've any problem, let me know.'

'Right, sir,' he said, and he went out.

Angel turned to Cartlett. 'Now then, sir—'

Cartlett said, 'Look you here, Angel, I am an American citizen, and at home I am welcomed and fêted and looked up to by everybody. I come to this damned freezing hell of a country and have somehow been involved in the death of a famous woman, which has nothing at all to do with me. I'm a guest in this goddamn country, but the way I have been treated, I might just as well be a bum on the backstreets of Baltimore. Now the latest insult is that you want to vacuum me. Isn't that what you do to carpets and drapes?'

'Well, sir, I am sorry for any discourtesy that you may think has been shown to you, but you will understand that we are trying to find out who murdered Joan Minter. And as the officer in charge, I have to—'

'All I understand, mister, is that I have an important meeting tomorrow in Beverley Hills, and I simply must be there. My studio is negotiating with a prominent author and a famous actor to make an outstanding motion picture through 2015. As chairman of the board I simply have to be there. The result of these negotiations will affect the employment of two hundred and sixty men and women for the next year or so. There are a lot of family's futures wrapped up in this deal.'

'I would like nothing better than to be able to release you, but you were present at a murder and I must extract from you every possible piece of information I can before I can do that. I trust that the members of your board can deal with the negotiations in your absence.'

The American was furious. His face was scarlet. He ran his hand through his hair and rose to his feet. 'You've not heard a word I've said. I must contact the American Embassy.'

'Please sit down, Mr Cartlett,' Angel said.

'I will not sit down. I am not prepared to be put off by a load of double talk.'

Angel was quite unmoved by the attitude of the American. He dipped into his pocket and took out a small plastic box the size of a mobile phone and placed it on the table. 'I'd like to ask *you* a few questions. It's possible I might get from you all I need. This is a recording machine. I trust you have no objection to me recording the interview. It will save time making notes.'

Cartlett raised his eyebrows, leaned over Angel, offered a questioning gaze and said, 'You mean . . . I could be allowed to return to the States *today*?'

'It's possible,' Angel said. 'I'm not making any rash promises. You must be reasonable, Mr Cartlett. And try and see the situation from my point of view.'

Cartlett returned to the chair, sat down and breathed out a long sigh. He stroked his hair. He did this repeatedly. It seemed to have a soothing effect on him.

Angel rubbed his chin. 'It all depends upon scientific evidence, and the way the inquiry goes.'

'Well, let's move it along then, Inspector, *please*.'

Angel nodded. 'Very well. What was your relationship with Miss Minter?'

Cartlett pursed his lips and his eyes narrowed. 'I was fond of her,' he said, 'and I think she liked me. We first met about 1974. That's forty years ago. It began when she was already a big name in the business. I was putting Shakespeare's *Romeo and Juliet* together to perform in the great cities of the world. I called it "The Great Cities Tour". I already had David Chesterfield as the male lead and was hoping to get Hannah

Lubrecki for Juliet, but it fell through. Now I knew that Joan was a great actress, but she didn't have the attraction Hannah had. Nevertheless, I wanted to sew this up quickly so I agreed a deal with Joan, who was wildly enthusiastic about playing Juliet opposite David Chesterfield. Thereafter she worked in my productions many, many times. She knew her strengths and always drove a hard bargain; but she was always excellent box office.'

'And, after all those years, what is your opinion of her now?' Angel said.

Cartlett shrugged. 'She was an actress and a businesswoman. I was a producer and a businessman. I still am. At the time she needed me, I needed her. We *had* to rub along together.'

'Have you any idea who might have hated her enough to want to murder her?'

Cartlett began stroking his hair again. Then he ran his fingers across his eyebrows before he said, 'Well no, Inspector. I cannot think of anybody who would be so wicked.'

Angel thought he had been very slow to answer. 'So, everybody loved Joan Minter, did they, Mr Cartlett?' he said.

'No. The film business is a tough business,' Cartlett said. 'Actors in particular need the hide of an elephant to withstand all the battering that goes on. They need to know how to be two-faced, to conceal their real feelings and to be able to say that they love everybody and everybody loves them. That's why they're known as "loveys". Take Felix Lubrecki, for example, son of the famous Hannah Lubrecki. After the business of Joan being cast as Juliet all those years back, Joan made the point to the media that she *took* the part from Hannah. *That* suggested to the outside world that the studio thought that Joan was a better actress than the great Hannah Lubrecki was. That was far from the truth. And *that* made Hannah depressed. She was also out of work for a few months. It set her on a downward spiral. She took to the bottle. Someone — possibly Joan, but I don't know for certain — put it around that she was an alcoholic, which also wasn't true. But that was another reason why the offer of star roles stopped going her way. Eventually she died in a poor way in a flat in London somewhere. But Hannah was a magnificent actress. And such beauty you rarely saw. Those Polish cheekbones . . . some women would die for. She was far more beautiful and superior to Joan Minter's chocolate-box beauty. So you can hardly expect Felix to feel kindly disposed towards Joan, can you? Yet, here he is, being offered, and apparently cheerfully accepting, her hospitality. But you don't have to tell Felix that you heard all this about his mother from me.'

Angel raised his eyebrows. 'Thank you for that,' he said. 'I'll bear it in mind when I speak to Mr Lubrecki.'

Then he looked at his notes. 'Do you own a firearm?' he said.

'I have a shotgun and a revolver at home.'

'You didn't bring the revolver with you, did you?'

'No, sir.'

'Tell me exactly what happened when you were listening to Joan Minter speaking from the top of the grand piano.'

'Sure. She was having a great time. She had a glass in one hand and a cigarette in the other. I think she had had a drop or two more of champagne than she should have. She made a side-swipe at her four ex-husbands and was recalling the beginning of her career at a kid's competition somewhere locally when the lights in the room went out and a gun close by me went off.'

'How near were you to the gun?'

'A couple of yards, I guess. Then the door was opened.'

'How near were you to the door?'

'Three yards, I guess.'

'Then what happened?'

'The gunman, I assume, went out, crossed the hall and went out of the front door.'

'Did the light from the hall show into the room while the door was open?'

'No. The hall light must have been switched off.'

'Before the shooting, did you see anybody in the room you didn't know?'

'No. But I wasn't taking a roll call.'

'And after the shooting, did you notice anybody missing?'

'No. But *someone* definitely went out. I wasn't inclined to chase after him because he had a gun. A second or two later the front door banged.'

'Didn't the light from the gun flash illuminate the person with the gun?'

'Not to me. I was in front of it.'

'What makes you think it was a man?'

'I dunno. I guess it seems the most likely gender to be toting a gun around. I know that women can use a gun these days, but . . .' He shrugged and left the sentence unfinished.

Angel nodded.

There was a knock at the door.

Angel looked round. 'Come in,' he called.

It was Ahmed. He was carrying a sheet of A4 and a laptop.

'Good morning, sir,' he said, then he saw Erick Cartlett. 'Oh, good morning, sir. Am I interrupting anything?'

Cartlett glared at him.

Angel said, 'Come in, lad. Sit down.' He looked at the sheet of A4 Ahmed was carrying, assumed it was for him and held out his hand.

Ahmed passed it to him. 'It's an email, sir. Came in just as I was leaving. It's from Records.'

'Take your coat off and sit down,' Angel said, then he looked at the email.

It said:

Walther PPK/S.32 automatic. Number 22394297
2 July 1969, one of an order for twenty from Carl Walther GmbH, Ulm, West Germany by Dienst Specialistische Recherche Toepassingen (Special Investigative Services) Dutch Police, The Hague, Netherlands. 17/22 February 1973, was lost while in service in Amsterdam.

7 January 1975, was found in the possession of Michael Stuart McCoy, by Metropolitan Police, UK.
22 August 1976, McCoy sentenced at Old Bailey for eight years for armed robbery.
30 August 2000, delivered to RASC Cardiff for secure storage.
2 February 2001, stolen from RASC Cardiff with other weapons.
Present location unknown.

Angel became aware that Cartlett was tapping his foot on the carpet. He looked up at him.

The muscles round the American's face were drawn tight.

Cartlett stared at his watch then said, 'I hope you haven't forgotten about me.'

Angel sighed. He put the sheet of A4 on the table. 'This is some valuable information about the gun that we believe was the murder weapon.'

'I am not interested in *that*,' Cartlett said. 'When are you going to permit me to leave?'

Angel's lips tightened. 'Not before I have the results of the gunshot residue test, sir. And maybe not even then. It depends on what it shows. Now, I have all that I need from you, Mr Cartlett — for the time being. I suggest you wait in your room so that I can reach you quickly.'

Cartlett's eyes flashed. His face was scarlet. He leaped to his feet. 'Dear *God*!' he said. Then he stomped across the room to the door, snatched it open, went out and closed it with a bang.

Ahmed turned to Angel with a quizzical look.

'He's been nothing but trouble,' Angel said. 'I don't trust him.'

He reached out, picked up the miniature recording machine, pressed the playback button and handed it to Ahmed. 'Tap that out. It's the interview with him.'

'Right, sir,' Ahmed said as he unzipped the laptop case.

'I'm ready to continue with the interviews and I want you to take down the witnesses' replies.'

'I'll do it directly onto here, sir,' he said, indicating the laptop, 'if that's all right. It saves time.'

'Right. First of all, find me a man called Felix Lubrecki. He's about forty, slim, black hair. He is a guest here. If you're stuck ask DS Taylor or DS Carter.'

'Right, sir,' Ahmed said, and he left the room.

THREE

As he waited for Felix Lubrecki, Angel picked up the email about the Walther PPK/S.32. He leaned back in the chair and reread it while rubbing his chin. He was thinking that as the gun was found on the lawn directly opposite the front door of the house, it suggested that after the murderer had shot Joan Minter, he or she had left the drawing room, crossed the hall, gone out through the front door, run straight across the drive onto the lawn and deliberately or accidently dropped the gun while making good their escape on the way to the main gate. If that were so, whether it was a guest or an intruder, the murderer would *not* be among the gathering remaining, which was all very confusing. Was he looking for a murderer among the wrong band of suspects? Should he start looking at the four ex-husbands? Should he therefore allow Erick Cartlett to return to the States? These were some of the problems that troubled him. He squeezed the lobe of his ear between a finger and thumb.

There was a knock at the door.

Angel said, 'Come in.'

It was Ahmed. He put his head round the door. 'I've found Mr Lubrecki, sir,' he said.

'Right. Come on in,' Angel said.

Ahmed stood back and let Felix Lubrecki enter the room in front of him.

'You wanted to see me, Inspector?' he said.

Angel nodded. 'Please sit down, Mr Lubrecki. Yes, I am interviewing all the guests at Miss Minter's party individually.' He put his hand out to indicate Ahmed and said, 'And DC Ahaz here is taking notes.'

Lubrecki nodded.

After asking for Mr Lubrecki's address and telephone number, Angel said, 'You must have been a very good friend of Miss Minter to have been invited to this special party?'

'I'm not sure that I would have regarded myself as a *very* good friend, Inspector. She was appreciably older than I am. My mother, Hannah Lubrecki, was a contemporary of hers and in earlier days knew her well.'

'Were they good friends, then?' Angel said craftily.

The question made Lubrecki hesitate. His eyes shot rapidly from left to right and back again. He licked his bottom lip then said, 'Erm . . . not exactly, no.'

Angel put his hands together to form a steeple then slowly interlocked the fingers. He pursed his lips, looked at him across the table and raised his eyebrows.

Lubrecki said, 'Well, Inspector, my mother was a very beautiful woman, particularly when she was in her twenties and thirties. You may say that I am prejudiced, but I've seen her in films of the sixties and seventies.'

'So have I, Mr Lubrecki,' Angel said. 'I can unhesitatingly confirm what you say. She was most . . . erm, alluring.'

'And Joan was jealous of her success,' he said. 'My mother was offered a leading role in a blockbuster part, which she accepted. Joan got to hear of it and, using her womanly wiles, somehow got the producer to change his mind. My mother wasn't told that Joan had got the part instead of her. She was amazed to read about it in the newspapers with a quote by Joan saying that she had got the part in straight competition with Hannah Lubrecki. This wasn't true and did my mother great harm. Anyway, they had a big row the next time they met. Thereafter, there was always a coldness between them. Of course, my mother still got offers of parts, but never the big remunerative roles she had been used to getting.'

Angel nodded. Then he said, 'Well, why would Miss Minter invite you, then?'

'Oh, well, I played her infant son in an early film called *Beware My Vision*. She was very kind to me. She said I was the son she never had. Over the years, our paths crossed frequently, and I was in many of the films she was in. Never the lead. Never in the glorious superstrata that she enjoyed. But there I was, third or fourth or sixth or tenth down the list of credits.'

'I see,' Angel said. 'So *you* were on very good terms with Miss Minter?'

'I wouldn't even put it as strong as that, Inspector. This is a dog-eat-dog profession, and it is better to have a short memory rather than a long one. Being ostensibly on good terms with Joan and being seen with her over the years has stood me in good stead for getting more work by simply being in the public eye.'

'Thank you. I understand. Was there anybody else who held a grudge against Miss Minter?'

Lubrecki rubbed his chin. 'I'm afraid there would be quite a few people. Of course, so much of it is wicked gossip initiated by sour grapes.'

'Well, tell me. Let me decide.'

Lubrecki's forehead creased. 'Well, there's the story about Perdita Gold.'

Angel's eyebrows went up.

Lubrecki noticed and said, 'Oh? I see you know who I mean.'

'Oh yes,' Angel said. 'Another very stunning woman. Occasionally seen as an oriental princess or queen in romantic love stories. Very beautiful, she was.'

'You wouldn't have thought she was so beautiful if you saw her arriving at Shepperton at six o'clock on a January morning with her hair in a towel.'

Angel smiled.

'Anyway,' Lubrecki said, 'Perdita was promised top billing when writer/director Karl Hartmann offered her a part in *Valley of Desire*. When the publicity went out her name was *under* that of Joan's. Worse than that, she was cast as Joan Minter's character's sister and Perdita is more than twenty years *younger* than Joan. When Perdita challenged all this, Joan said that those conditions were written into her contract. Perdita stuck it out and made the film but said that subsequently it held her back from getting some parts and the money was much less. That was a long time ago. But she remembers having to do a live pier show in the South of England somewhere during the summer of 2000 to make ends meet.'

'Were Miss Minter and Perdita Gold sworn enemies, then?'

'I wouldn't go that far, Inspector. But, of course, if Perdita *had* been invited to this party here, she didn't turn up, did she?'

'Is there anybody here who was involved in that story?'

'Yes. There's Leo Altman. He had a small part in the film. Which reminds me of another story about Leo Altman and Joan, which doesn't show Joan up in a good light.'

Angel nodded. 'Please tell me about it.'

Lubrecki said, 'Well, there was a young film-maker called Charles Fachinno, who had an option on a screenplay of the bestselling novel, *Dawn Never Comes*. He wanted Joan Minter and Leo Altman for the leading parts. Joan read it, liked it and phoned to say that she'd like to do it. They talked money, agreed a deal and a contract was being drawn up. At the same time, with funds borrowed from a bank, Fachinno bought the screenplay for a quarter of a million pounds. Then Joan gave back word. Because she gave back word, the leading man, Leo Altman, also gave back word. The story was reported in a society magazine and nobody would look at Fachinno's project after that. It looked as if Joan had rejected it because she had considered it wasn't a commercial proposition. Fachinno owed the bank. He appealed to Joan, told her the situation; she said that as she hadn't signed anything, it was hard lines. She had been offered double the money in the comedy, *Find the Lady*, which turned out to be a huge success. Fachinno said that she had made it worse by letting word get out that she had declined the part. He had thought he could trust her. Anyhow, it bankrupted the man. Also, Leo Altman never had a leading part offered again. He had to be content with bit parts of butlers or doctors. He crawled about after Joan Minter pretending to take sides with her. He had been hoping that Joan would sometimes put in a good word for him, but she never did.'

Angel knew he would have to see Leo Altman to get his version of the story.

'Thank you, Mr Lubrecki. Those backstage happenings are quite . . . um, enlightening.'

'I hope they prove helpful in your enquiries, Inspector.'

'I hope so too. Now can we turn to the murder yesterday? Where were you when Miss Minter was making her speech and was shot?'

'I was several feet in front of the man with the gun.'

'What makes you think it was a man?'

'I don't know. There wasn't a sound or anything to indicate it was a woman. Maybe it was because there was no rustling sound from his clothes. If it had been a woman, there might have been. There were no smells of paint, powder or perfume emanating from him either.'

Angel blinked. It was unusual to hear such a police-like answer from a witness. 'Thank you,' Angel said.

He was slowly coming to the belief that, indeed, the murderer must have been a man.

'Just a couple more questions, Mr Lubrecki. I take it you knew all the people present in the room before Miss Minter was shot?'

'Yes, indeed.'

'Well, after Miss Minter was shot, did you notice who was missing?'

'Well, no . . . I didn't notice.'

'Pity,' Angel said.

Angel continued the interviews after lunch. He knew that he must try to finish them that day so he would have to get a move on.

Ahmed ushered Mr Leo Altman into the room and when he was comfortably settled at the table opposite Angel, the inspector said, 'Yours is a well-known face to me, Mr Altman. You seem hardly ever to be off our screens these days.'

The grey-haired gentleman nodded and said, 'Then you must be watching old films, Inspector.'

'I suppose I am,' he said.

'That sounds almost like a compliment.'

'It was intended to be,' Angel said with a smile. 'Now, I'm anxious to know what your relationship was with Miss Minter.'

'Well, we had known each other a very long time. She probably knew me as well or better than anybody else here. I had a great respect for her. She had worked and battled her way to the top of her profession.'

'Were you envious of her standing? You said that you had known her a *very* long time?'

'Not at all.'

'I wondered if you felt that Lady Luck had not been kind to you.'

'You could say that, Inspector. Success in this business is made up of three things: talent, judgement and being in the right place at the right time.'

'And what caused the disaster of the project *Dawn Never Comes*?'

Altman shuffled uneasily in the chair. He rubbed his chin. 'Fancy you knowing about that.'

Angel said, 'You were going to be the star in that film, weren't you?'

'Yes, I was. It was a long time ago. It was a great story and a great part for me.'

'What happened? The film was never made, was it?'

'No, it never was. Everything that could have gone wrong did go wrong.'

'But it needn't have happened, need it?'

'No. It was a great shame. It came when I was just beginning to break through from minor parts to leads.'

'Tell me about it,' Angel said. 'What happened?'

'Well . . . a young man, new to the film business, got an option on the book *Dawn Never Comes* and he started to set it all up. He wanted me as the male lead and Joan as female lead. A film was about ten weeks' work and tremendous exposure thereafter round the world. I thought, if it's good enough for Joan, it would be good enough for me. His name was Charles Fachinno. I'd never heard of him. He'd been a big wheel in the potted-meat business. All those little glass jars. You don't see them these days. Well, who eats potted meat these days? Anyway, he sent me a screenplay, which I thought was outstanding. My agent worked out a deal which was highly satisfactory and I was ready to sign a contract, when I got a message that Joan had changed her mind. That made me a bit nervous. Well, very nervous. Then I began to think about the situation. Fachinno was unknown to us. Being successful in the potted-meat business wasn't any recommendation for producing what I thought was going to be a major film. Also, I had no idea who the director was going to be. It's important to have someone in that job that you've confidence in. So I didn't sign and I returned the contract unsigned.'

'Then what happened?'

'All hell broke loose. One of those glossy magazines came along and Joan gave them the story that she'd no faith in the new blockbuster film that was being talked about. She told them that she didn't know anything about the "potted-meat man". He was in a business he didn't know about. She said the screenplay was amateurish and boys'-own. She rubbished it so much that I was embarrassed. Then I heard Charles Fachinno had been to see her but she had been very rude to him. On the strength of getting a verbal agreement from her that she would take the female lead, Fachinno had put his potted-meat business as security and got the bank to shell out a quarter of a million to the author and a commitment to shell out further sums. But now Fachinno couldn't make the film because Joan had so compellingly disparaged the project. I wasn't pleased because my name had been associated with what was now becoming regarded as a flop. Coincidentally, or maybe because of it, I was out of work and had not a single job in my diary. I was becoming quite desperate . . . almost at the stage of getting out of the business, when I saw an ad in *The Stage* for auditions for the part of a butler in a new play called *Find the Lady* starring, surprisingly, Joan Minter. I was amazed and resentful that she had come out of the mess so well, the mess that she had helped to create. I really had to eat humble pie to get that job as butler. And have been butlers, doctors, hotel clerks and judges ever since. I never did get a lead offered after that.'

'But you've never been out of work, have you?'

'That's true.'

'Now about yesterday. Can you tell me where you were standing just before Miss Minter was shot?'

'I was in front of the man with the gun. I was standing between Felix Lubrecki and Erick Cartlett.'

'Were you far from the door?'

'About six or eight feet.'

'I take it you knew everybody in the room?'

'Yes. Everybody except Joan's staff: her secretary, the butler and the caterers.'

'Yes, of course. Could you say who *wasn't* there after Miss Minter had been shot and the lights were turned back on?'

'No. I never thought to look. It was all too dreadful . . .'

FOUR

It was 4 p.m. Angel was still interviewing the guests and staff of the Mansion House, and eliciting unexpected information about the personal and working life of Joan Minter. He was at the table in the little sitting room, rubbing his chin. But he wasn't any clearer as to the identity of her murderer.

There was a knock on the door. It was Ahmed. 'I've got Mrs Bell, sir,' he said.

'Come in, Mrs Bell,' Angel said.

The young woman with the shining, wet eyes said, 'It's *Miss* Bell, Inspector, actually. But please call me Jane.'

'Right . . . er . . . Jane. Please sit down.'

'Thank you,' she said, wiping her cheek with a tissue.

Angel waited. He contented himself looking at her and smiling to try to put her at ease.

She looked up at him and said, 'Excuse me, may I ask if you are *the* Inspector Angel, the one in the papers that they say is like the Canadian Mounties because he always gets his man?'

Ahmed smiled as he watched Angel's reaction.

The inspector was always embarrassed at this question and wanted to get it quickly out of the way. 'Well, yes. I suppose I am.'

'I've seen you on the television, I'm sure. They say that you've always solved the murder cases you've been given. I read it in a paper or a magazine somewhere.'

'Yes, well . . . I do what I have to do.'

Her eyes filled up again. 'I'm sorry,' she said. 'I just can't control myself. I've never been so close to a . . . to somebody who died.'

Angel knew the feeling well. After all, over the years he had had to deal with many tragedies involving all kinds of people including mature men, sometimes some of whom broke down in tears, both genuine and false. If the dead person was known to be a villain, of course it wasn't difficult to remain controlled and level-headed. But sometimes it wasn't easy for a young woman, not much older than a girl, to control her emotions.

'Well, you're not to worry, Jane.'

'Well, I do worry, Inspector. I'm afraid. I know that the murderer is here among us. I don't know who I can trust.'

'*How* do you know?'

'Stands to reason, Inspector. Nobody saw a stranger in the dining room or anywhere in the house. Nobody has come forward and said that they saw a stranger. There is no stranger. If there is no stranger, then the murderer must be one of the guests. If a guest wants to murder Miss Minter, an icon and one of the nicest ladies in the world, well, there's no telling who else he might want to murder. He might want to murder me. Well, I've never done anybody any harm . . . not knowingly, anyway. And if I had, I would certainly want to apologize and put it right.'

Angel nodded. 'At the moment, Jane, it seems that there *was* a stranger in the house,' he said. 'That he crept in behind everybody while you were watching Miss Minter giving her speech from the top of the piano. That he chose his time, switched off the lights, shot her, then let himself out by the front door and disappeared into the night.'

'I think a strange face among that crowd of celebrities would be bound to have been recognized by one of them and reported, Inspector. I certainly didn't see anybody.'

'Jane, I said that it *seemed* that a stranger crept into the place. I didn't say I agreed with it.'

'But, Inspector, I didn't know until just now that the gun that killed her had been found, and that it had been found on the lawn on the way to the main gate. Surely that's evidence that it *was* a stranger making his escape after all?'

'Not at all,' Angel said. 'All the murderer had to do was go upstairs to the first floor, go into the bathroom or the lavatory, lock the door and throw the gun out of the window. You wouldn't have to be a medal winner at the Olympics to manage that. Any old biddy would have been able to do that.'

She looked at Angel, and sighed. 'Oh. Oh yes,' she said with a smile. The smile quickly faded. A hand went up to her face. 'That means that the murderer is still here. It's somebody in the house, then!'

It was 5 p.m.

Angel was still in the small sitting room at the Mansion House. He had let Ahmed cadge a lift to the police station in the SOCO van. Angel would like to have called it a day himself and gone home but there was still one interview that wouldn't wait.

There was a knock at the door.

Angel quickly took the small recording machine out of his pocket, switched it to record and put it on the desk in front of him.

'Come in,' he called.

'Ah, Mr Trott,' Angel said. 'Come in. Please sit down. I understand that you wanted to see me?'

'I'll stand, sir. If you don't mind,' Trott said. 'Yes, sir. It's an organizational and financial matter.'

Angel frowned and looked at him closely.

'Mr and Mrs Jones, the caterers, are still here feeding the guests and they should be paid,' Trott said. 'And they need to know how much longer they are required to be here. After all, they were only contracted to supply and serve four meals, three yesterday and one today. They've already been here two nights. All the guests are still here and have to be catered for.'

Angel's eyes narrowed. '*Two* nights?' he said.

'They came Saturday to check out the facilities, the electric sockets for their cooking equipment and hotplates and the layout of the rooms and so on. They now need to restock with victuals. They cannot manage any longer without going to the market and they also need some money to be able to pay for what is needed. The question is, how much longer are they to be here, and who is going to pay them? In addition, the house being full of guests, I am now also urgently in need of the services of a housekeeper and a chambermaid. I cannot on my own maintain the standard of cleanliness and service that Miss Minter would have expected from me.'

'Well, Mr Trott, it really has nothing to do with me. If the guests were not eating and sleeping here, they would be eating and sleeping *some*where. It just happens that they were away from home when this murder occurred. I think this matter should be worked out between Miss Bell, you, the Joneses and the guests. Perhaps each guest would like to pay an appropriate sum for their keep, or maybe Miss Bell has access to some petty cash of Miss Minter's. I really have no other suggestions to make.'

The corners of Trott's mouth turned downward. 'Thank you, sir,' he said without conviction. 'Could you say how much longer it will be necessary for the guests to remain here?'

Angel wrinkled his forehead, then sighed and rubbed his chin. 'I believe that I have now seen everybody. I am only waiting for the gunshot residue results from Wetherby lab, which could be here sometime tomorrow.'

'Very well, sir,' he said. 'That does mean we will have to manage another two meals and another night at least. I shall immediately convene a meeting between the parties you suggest and see what can best be done. Thank you, sir.'

He turned towards the door.

Angel said, 'Mr Trott?'

He turned back.

Angel said, 'I seem to have overlooked a question I should have asked you earlier.'

'What's that, sir?'

'When Miss Minter was on the piano addressing the guests, just before she was shot, was the front door locked?'

'I have to confess, sir, that I don't actually know. It should have been, but as I did not check it myself I don't expect that it was.'

'I'll take it that it was *not* locked, then.'

Trott nodded, looking forlorn.

Angel said, 'In the drawing room, you were standing quite close to the piano, weren't you?'

'I was, sir.'

'So you had a similar view of the guests to that that Miss Minter had?'

He pursed his lips. 'Well, yes, sir.'

'Was there a stranger, a person who should not have been there or anybody you didn't know among the guests listening to her?'

'I didn't see anybody, sir, but you will understand my eyes were more on Miss Minter than the guests. I was concerned that she did not fall. The piano was highly polished and she was standing on the top in very slippery silk stockings.'

Angel sighed. 'Right, thank you, Mr Trott.'

The butler went out and closed the door.

Angel pulled a face. None of Trott's answers had actually been helpful. He looked at his watch. It was 5.15 p.m. He had had enough. It was time he was going home.

Angel arrived home at 5.35 p.m. He locked the BMW in the garage, walked quickly along the path to the back door and let himself in. The door opened straight into the kitchen. It was warm and a pleasant smell of cooking pervaded the kitchen. The lids of two pans on the gas oven were rattling, giving out a lot of steam. He peered down at the rings, turned them down a little, then noticed a light showing through the glass door of the oven. He could see a casserole dish inside. He smiled, then pursed his lips and began to blow a tune through his teeth. It was vaguely like 'I Feel Pretty' from *West Side Story*. He reached into the fridge for a can of German beer, found a tumbler in the cupboard and poured some out. He took a sip, nodded approvingly, then ambled into the hall. He looked in the sitting room. There was nobody in there. He went to the bottom of the steps and called out.

'Mary. Mary.'

'Coming, love,' she called.

'Are you all right, darling?' he said.

Mary came to the top of the stairs. 'You're early,' she said as she ran down.

She was smiling.

He looked at her and thought she looked as alluring and desirable as the day they were married.

He glanced at his watch. 'Am I?' he said.

They kissed. It was just a peck.

'Any post?' he said.

'On the sideboard,' she said as she made for the kitchen. 'It's always on the sideboard.'

Angel screwed up his face. He went into the sitting room. On the sideboard he saw a colourful envelope. He reached out for it. 'I know it's always on the sideboard,' he said, 'except when it's in your coat pocket, between the pages of your library book, behind the clock, on the kitchen table or in your handbag.'

'Oh. I've had a letter from Miriam,' she said.

Angel ambled into the kitchen and tore into the colourful envelope he had picked up. 'Where is it? What does she want *this* time?'

'I've got it. I want to talk to you about it.'

Angel pinched the bridge of his nose and squeezed his eyes. 'Oh,' he groaned. 'What's the matter with her?'

Mary hesitated. She breathed in through her nose loudly to show her annoyance, then snappily she said, 'There's *nothing* the matter with her. You haven't read the letter and you are already making judgements.'

He sighed, turned away and took the letter out of the envelope he had just torn open. He quickly read it, sighed, then read it again. Then, holding it up to her, he said, 'What do you think?'

'Excuse me, love,' Mary said. 'Tea will be ready in a couple of minutes. Tell me about that later, do you mind? Would you like to set the table?'

He blinked. 'Eh? Oh yes. All right.'

He stuffed the letter back in its envelope and put it on the table. He opened a drawer in the kitchen table and took out some cork mats with hunting scenes on them, and the cutlery, and set them out. He stood up and took the cruet and the side plates from the cupboard, then put them also in position on the table.

'Thank you,' she said. 'Oh, it's lamb shanks. You might want the mint sauce.'

He turned back to the cupboard and found the mint sauce, then he rummaged around in the table drawer for a suitable spoon and put it by the jar.

Mary began serving out.

Angel stood up, took off his suit coat, went into the hall and hung it on the newel post. Then he returned to the kitchen rolling up his shirtsleeves. He ran the tap, found some soap and washed his hands enthusiastically.

Mary arrived at the sink with a pan of boiling cabbage and a colander. She looked at him and breathed in through her nose noisily. 'You could have done that job in the bathroom,' she said.

'I only want to wash my hands,' he said.

Angel reached out for the tea towel. Mary snatched it off him and pushed a hand towel at him.

'You could have done it earlier,' she said, pushing steaming potatoes onto the plates with a fork. 'Now sit down, out of the way,' she said.

Angel thoroughly enjoyed the lamb and afterwards the fresh raspberries and ice cream. He moved into the sitting room carrying two cups of coffee. He settled down in his favourite chair and reached out for the *Radio Times*. As he scanned the programme pages, he could hear Mary in the kitchen, banging pots and pans and slamming cupboard doors.

He couldn't find anything on the television he wanted to watch. He tossed the magazine to one side and called out, 'Your coffee's getting cold.'

'I'm coming,' she said.

He reached into his pocket, took out the letter, reread it and clenched his teeth. 'Huh!' he grunted.

Mary arrived. She quickly sat down in the other easy chair and lifted her feet onto the pouffe, then reached out to the library table and picked up the coffee cup and saucer. She took a sip, swallowed, smiled and said, 'Ah.'

She looked at the television screen, turned to Angel and said, 'Nothing on?'

'No.' He waved the letter he had been looking at. 'I want to talk to you about this.'

She wrinkled her nose. 'Let me show you Miriam's letter, first.'

He shrugged. 'If you want.'

She leaned forward, twisted round and took a blue handwritten envelope from behind a cushion.

Angel smiled. That was another place that *wasn't* the sideboard. He held his hand out.

Mary saw it. 'No,' she said. 'Let me read it to you.'

'I can read it myself,' he said. 'I've been able to read for years!'

'No. No. No.' She pulled out the single sheet of notepaper and began to read: '*Darlings,*

I do hope you are both OK and that that genius of a husband of yours isn't working too hard.

Both Katy and Will are doing well at school and often ask after you. The thing is, you remember saying that you'd like to come down for a few days? I said you are always welcome here, but I would especially like you to come down for a few days (or as long as you like) this week, if you can possibly manage it. You see, I have the chance of having my boobs done at forty per cent off early next Friday morning, the seventh. The surgeon has an open morning then, and Sarah, a girl I know who works there, told me about it. So I went to see him. The preliminary consultation was free, and he's ever so nice. He's measured me up and so on and the clinic is very up to date and sterilized and all that. I know several friends who have been there. And they look fantastic! But I need somebody to see that Katy and Will are safely taken to school and brought back and fed while I am sore. He said that would only last two or three days at most.

Anyway, let me know if you can manage it. If you can that would be absolutely marvellous. It will save me a fortune.

Love to you, my lovely sister, and bro-in-law — what would I do without you both?

Miriam. XXX

PS. Katy and Will can't wait to see you.'

Mary put her hand with the letter in it down on her lap and said, 'What can I do?'

Angel wasn't pleased. He ran his hand through his hair. Then moistened his lips. 'It's a long way up to Edinburgh, but you'll have to go, I suppose,' he said.

Mary nodded. 'I knew you'd say that.'

Angel wrinkled his nose.

She said, 'You could be more gracious about it.'

'*Gracious?*' he said. He opened his mouth to say something, then thought better of it.

'Is it all right, then? Will you able to manage? If I thought for one moment you wouldn't be able to manage, I wouldn't go.'

'I'll manage,' he said. 'Of course, I'll manage. I've managed before. But your sister's a pain in the backside. Ever since she kicked that poor bloke out, she's—'

'What poor bloke? You mean Angus?'

'No. That painter-and-decorator chap.'

'He was an architect. You mean Francois?'

'No, her husband. The first one. Rupert, or whatever his name was.'

'You mean Robert? That was her *first* husband. Rupert McGee was her solicitor at the time. He was dreadful. They both were.'

'*He* was all right. If he hadn't caught her messing about with that painter and decorator, they could have still been together.'

'He was an architect. Oh, it's a long story. There's a lot more to it than that. He was dreadful. The things he said to her.'

'She wasn't exactly incapable of dishing out a tongue-lashing, was she?!'

Mary sniffed, then said, 'Trust you to be pulling her to pieces.'

There was a pause in the exchange while Angel finished off his coffee and put the cup and saucer on the library table.

'Well, I hope that when she's parading her new equipment up and down Princes Street, she pulls a bloke as loopy as she is, who will put up with her crackpot schemes and idiotic ideas.'

Mary's face went scarlet. She whipped her feet off the pouffe and stood up. She leaned over and snatched up Angel's cup and said, 'I hope you don't want any more coffee, because there isn't any.'

Then she stormed off into the kitchen.

Angel's watched her go, his mouth wide open and his forehead creased.

Then he heard the running of water and more banging of pots and pans.

He pulled the envelope containing the letter that had been addressed to him out of his pocket. He looked down at it, clenched his teeth while rubbing the back of his neck for a few seconds, then stuffed it back in his pocket.

FIVE

The next morning, Tuesday, 4 November 2014, three miles or so from Bromersley, on a country lane leading to the A1, concealed behind a hawthorn hedge was a Volkswagen Jetta. The car had had all its windows removed.

The driver was wearing a black balaclava underneath a fibreglass helmet, which was securely fastened under his chin, a pair of heavy-duty gloves and thick plastic knee, ankle, elbow and wrist supports over a dark suit. He looked at his watch. It was 8.38 a.m. He started the engine and pressed down the accelerator several times. The car responded with lionlike roars. The vehicle had been checked out most carefully the night before.

The mobile phone on the shelf in front of him rang out. He snatched it up.

'Yeah?' he said.

'Just going under the railway arches,' a voice said. 'Right behind him. Everything OK?'

'Yeah,' the driver said. 'Should be visible to you in about sixty seconds.'

The phone went dead.

The driver threw down the phone, shuffled in his seat, revved the car engine again and gazed down the road. He snatched up a pair of binoculars, lifted up his eye shield and peered through them. There was nothing. The road was empty. Then he looked again. He could now see something on the narrow, twisting road. A big blue and white van. It had writing on the side. *That was the van!* A good two hundred yards behind it he saw the blue Ford Mondeo. His heart banged away like a drum. He breathed faster.

He kept his eye on the van. It was travelling fast. Too fast, he thought.

The security van driver had to stop at a halt sign to turn left into the main road north to the A1. The Volkswagen Jetta was waiting up a dirt-track lane, behind a hawthorn hedge, fifty yards away. The driver revved the car one more time, then released the handbrake, let in the clutch and began travelling down the lane. He had to match his speed so that they both arrived at the halt sign together, hopefully with his wheels travelling faster than fifty miles per hour.

He still thought the van was travelling too fast. He pressed the car accelerator down further. The engine responded. The speedometer showed sixty miles per hour. He thought he was on target. The van showed its side view to him. 'Slater Security,' it read. It was slowing down. That was good. His speed was sixty-five miles per hour. He was two seconds away. He braced himself.

There was an unholy bang followed by the tearing and crunching of metal as the two vehicles became a mass of steaming and hissing scrap in the centre of the road.

A crowd of starlings flew noisily overhead, protesting at the disturbance.

There was a smell of scorched rubber. Liquids trickled onto the road, searching their way to the gutter.

Seconds later, the Ford Mondeo rolled in gently behind the pile up and stopped. Three men in balaclavas leaped out of the car, wielding pickaxes and heavy hammers. They raced towards the back doors of the van and began to dismantle them with their weapons.

Meanwhile, the big driver of the Volkswagen managed to kick open the car's door, which had compacted into the door jamb. He disentangled himself from the wreckage, glanced at the point of impact of the two vehicles, grinned, then pulled out a Beretta handgun from his pocket as he ran round to the offside of the security van to take the driver and his mate in hand. They were still in their seats, shaking their heads and blinking. He saw a red button on the dashboard flashing.

'Oh, *hell*!' the driver of the Volkswagen said.

That was the button to be pressed by the driver in an emergency. It transmitted by radio a pre-recorded distress message with an added map reference to the security firm's depot. The car driver had hoped to have prevented the call being sent. He quickly looked round for the aerial. He saw two. He reached out and hammered each of them savagely at the base with the butt of the handgun, then grabbed them and yanked them off the vehicle, hoping that he had been able to stop the signal to the security company in time.

The van driver and his mate looked round and saw him. He waved the gun at them. They saw it and put up their hands.

'Take your helmets off, leave them there and get out,' he said.

They slowly obeyed.

He pointed the gun at a space on the pavement and said, 'Lie down there on your bellies, close your eyes, don't move and you won't get hurt. I'll be watching you.'

He then looked towards the back of the van to see what was happening. Suddenly, the three men in balaclavas, jeans and T-shirts jumped out of the van. One of them was trailing a flex of wire and a battery.

'Take cover,' he called.

The men ran back about fifteen yards, then squatted on the road with their backs to the van.

The big man with the gun ran with them.

The man trailing the wire called out, 'Heads down. Three. Two. One. Blast!'

There was a loud explosion in the back of the van, creating a small cloud of white smoke.

The men dashed back into the van. There was a quiet moment, then a small cheer went up followed by a lot of activity. The big man in the dark suit went to the Ford Mondeo, removed a brown and white suitcase and took it to the van. Three minutes later, the four gang members and the suitcase, bursting with money, were in the Ford Mondeo, which was being cautiously driven at a steady thirty miles an hour back towards Bromersley town centre. The driver took the road out of town to Cheapo's supermarket car park, where they left the car discreetly parked among sixty or seventy other cars and made their different ways to their own transport. The big man took the brown and white suitcase.

It was 8.28 a.m. when Angel arrived at his office the following morning, Tuesday, 4 November 2014. He was quickly followed by PC Ahmed Ahaz, whose eyebrows were raised and eyes were shining. 'Have you seen this, sir?' he said, holding a newspaper out in front of him.

Angel's mind was fully engrossed in the murder case and on what he needed urgently to attend to that morning. He didn't intend being diverted. 'What is it, Ahmed?' he said tetchily.

'The front four pages are all about the Joan Minter case, sir.'

'Well, she was very famous, there's bound to be . . . *Four* pages, did you say?'

'And there's a photograph of you, sir, on page two.'

He lowered his eyebrows. '*Me?*' he growled. He took the paper and glanced at the front page. It was the *Daily Yorkshireman*. The headline was: 'Joan Minter murder official: Angel leading investigation.' There were two photographs of her on her own, a very early one and a most recent one; four with her and her respective husband at the time, and an old photograph of Angel looking smart in uniform when he was a police sergeant.

He blinked when he saw the picture of himself. He glanced at the other pages, then turned to Ahmed and said, 'Can I read this later, Ahmed?'

Unusually, Ahmed hesitated. 'Yes, sir,' he said, 'but can I have it back because I want to put it in my scrapbook.'

Angel concealed a smile. 'Yes, of course,' he said. 'I won't forget.'

Ahmed looked pleased and made for the door.

Angel said, 'Find Trevor Crisp for me, will you?' His face muscles tightened, then he shook his head. 'I can never find that lad.'

'Righto, sir. I think he's in CID,' Ahmed said, and he went out.

A few moments later, DS Crisp arrived.

Being the head of CID at Bromersley, Angel wanted to be briefed about crimes reported to CID the previous day while he had been busy on the Joan Minter murder.

Crisp had dealt with most of the matters of importance. He told Angel that he had shown Mrs Sellars their rogues' gallery but that she had been unable to identify the crook who had taken her attention while his accomplice had stolen her handbag. He also reported all he could about the theft of the two cars from Mr and Mrs Sellars.

The phone rang.

Angel reached out for it. It was DS Taylor. 'The results of the gunshot residue tests have just arrived by courier, sir.'

Angel said, 'Well, bring them down. I want to know what they say!'

He slammed down the phone and turned back to Crisp.

The phone rang again.

Angel frowned at it, then snatched it up. It was the station civilian telephone receptionist, Mrs Meredew. 'There's an emergency call from Slater Security on the line, sir.'

'Put them through,' he said.

A man said, 'We've had a brief automated emergency message from one of our vans, two or three miles away from you. It's at a crossroads between the villages of Hemmsfield and Indale. They were making their way south to join the M1 south along Hemmsfield Road.'

Angel jumped to his feet. 'One moment, sir, please,' he said. He put a hand over the mouthpiece, turned to Crisp and said, 'Get Control to listen in to this and issue a red alarm.'

Crisp dashed out of the office.

Then Angel turned to the wall behind his desk that had a large map of the local area. In a second he had picked out the crossroads.

He removed his hand from the mouthpiece. 'A patrol car is on its way there now, sir,' he said. 'Our Control Room is being made aware of this emergency and is now sharing this call. The incident is at Bromersley Station map reference A1257 by K209. Have you contact with your van?'

'No. Both radio links with the van itself are dead. It's very unusual. Our communication manager is trying to raise them via the drivers' mobile phones.'

'If you succeed, advise our Control Room promptly and put them in the picture. What is your name?'

'I'm the manager here at the Leeds depot,' he said. 'Reader's my name, Mathew Reader.'

'Thank you, Mr Reader. We'll do what we can,' Angel said, and he replaced the phone.

Crisp came running in. 'Patrol car on the way, sir.'

Angel said, 'Right. Get out there. See what's happened. Then report to me.'

'Right, sir,' he said, and he went out.

Don Taylor caught the door. He was carrying several A4 sheets of paper. He knocked on it and said, 'Can I come in?'

Angel's eyebrows went up. 'Yes. Yes. Ah, the GSR results. What do they say, Don?'

Taylor looked down at the top sheet and said, 'I haven't read it myself yet, sir.'

Angel quietly said, 'Well, sit down, read it and tell me what it says.'

When he was settled, Taylor said. 'It says . . .'

He quickly broke off, turned over the first four pages to the last page and began to read again. 'It says the conclusions are . . . that of the persons tested for the presence of cartridge residue on their clothing, three of them had relatively large quantities. They are Felix Lubrecki, Leo Altman and Erick Cartlett. Also Alexander Trott was found to have minute traces of lead, antimony and barium in the sample submitted, which of course are the constituents of a bullet, which we found unusual. We suggest that the paraffin wax test be applied without delay to the four persons mentioned, which may immediately show up the person or persons who discharged a firearm up to seventy-two hours prior to the test being made.'

Angel looked at him and blinked. 'Is that it?' he said.

Taylor looked back at him. 'Yes, sir. The other pages are full of the safeguards that we should implement to prevent cross-infection. There are also long paragraphs saying that we shouldn't rely on the test too much and it should be used only to corroborate existing evidence of eye witnesses.'

Angel's eyebrows went skywards. 'We should be so lucky. Right, Don. Crack on with it, then. You know what we are looking for?'

'Blue specks with tails.'

'Especially on the thumb and forefinger.'

It was 9.30 a.m. before Angel could leave the station and resume his enquiries into the murder of Joan Minter. He pulled up outside the Mansion House on Ceresford Road where he was met at the door by a very angry Erick Cartlett. 'I have been waiting for you, sir. You have kept me here, hanging around the house, quite pointlessly causing me to miss a very important meeting. I have to warn you that I shall report your conduct in this matter to the American Embassy.'

Angel said, 'I'm sorry to have caused you any inconvenience, Mr Cartlett. Please come into Miss Minter's sitting room.'

Cartlett followed Angel into the little room off the hall that he was using as an office.

When Angel had closed the door, he turned to Cartlett and said, 'I have to point out to you, Mr Cartlett, that owing to the untimely death of your late friend, Miss Minter, *she* has also been very greatly inconvenienced and will be missing far more than *one* important meeting. Isn't it therefore reasonable that we should do our best to find whoever is responsible?'

Cartlett's jaw dropped. Then he said, 'Well, I am certainly not responsible. I now hear that I have to wait further for another indignity. A candle wax test, whatever that is.'

'It's *not* an indignity,' Angel said. 'It is merely the spreading of warm liquid paraffin wax on your hands and allowing it to harden. It's quite painless and it doesn't take long.'

'What's that supposed to prove?'

'The paraffin wax extracts from deep in the pores fine residues given off by the firing of a gun. We can see them in the hardened wax.'

Cartlett turned up his nose and said, 'But Joan was murdered about thirty-six hours ago. I've had a shower and a good soak in the bath since then. And washed my hands several times. Most of us have.'

'Doesn't matter. Washing your hands won't make any difference. The nitrates will be in your pores for up to seventy-two hours whether you've washed your hands or not.'

Cartlett's mood changed again. He straightened up and said, 'Well, what if I refuse?'

'Well, I hope you won't. It would very much look as if you're guilty. But, I suppose, if you refused, I should have to get a warrant.'

'Get a warrant, then.'

'There is another way,' Angel said.

Cartlett said, 'What's that?'

'I could put you under arrest for the murder of Joan Minter without the need for you to take the paraffin wax test. If you *are* guilty, it would show that it was a shrewd idea of mine. If you're innocent, it will hold you here in custody for at least another week, and I shan't have to worry about you absconding back home.'

Cartlett's mouth opened wide. His eyes narrowed. He scratched his temple and said, 'You wouldn't do that.'

'I might,' Angel said, 'so now will you go through to my sergeant and have the paraffin wax test? You'll not be alone. There are three other gentlemen before you . . .'

Meanwhile . . .

Crisp had arrived at the quiet T-junction, shortly after a Bromersley Police patrol car.

The two drivers of the Slater Security van were standing around with their hands in their pockets and stamping their feet on the pavement to keep warm. The police patrolmen had swiftly taped off the crashed vehicles, and had started erecting road signs indicating a detour.

Crisp had checked that the men in the security van were unharmed and noted what had happened. He took their names and addresses and asked them a few urgent questions, then phoned Angel on his mobile and reported the situation.

Angel said, 'Were either of the men able to give a description of any of the robbers and the getaway car?'

'They said there was nothing distinguishing about the robbers, sir, except that the one that spoke to them had a local accent,' Crisp said. 'They all wore black balaclavas. The car was a blue Ford Mondeo. It's come to me, sir, that the two cars involved would be the two cars stolen yesterday from Mr and Mrs Sellars on Ceresford Road.'

'So they were, Trevor. So they were. Did the robbers leave anything behind? Anything at all?'

'Just three pickaxes, sir.'

Angel rubbed his chin. 'Interesting . . . I'll send SOCO out and a photographer. And a low-loader to bring in the wrecks. Was there anything else? Anything at all? Anything that might give us a lead? An empty lager can, a glove, a piece of unburned detonator wire . . . anything?'

'Don't know, sir. Haven't been here long.'

'Well, have a good look round,' Angel said.

There was a knock on the sitting-room door.

'Hold on, Trevor,' Angel said. He put his hand over the mouthpiece. 'Come in,' he called. It was DS Carter.

'We've finished all our—' she began.

Angel pointed to the phone.

'Ooh, sorry, sir,' she said.

'Won't be a minute, Flora,' he said. 'Sit down.'

She nodded.

Then back into the phone he said, 'Well, have a good look round, Trevor. And keep all busy fingers away from the wreck. It's a crime scene. Preserve its integrity.'

'Of course. Righto, sir,' Crisp said.

Angel ended the call, closed his mobile and turned to DS Carter.

'Now then, Flora,' he said. 'What do you want?'

'We've finished our search, sir, and we've found nothing suspicious in any of the guests' rooms or the house or the perimeter of the house.'

'Hmmm,' Angel said, rubbing the back of his neck. 'Been through the rubbish bins?'

'Yes, sir, of course.'

He breathed out heavily. 'Very well. Dismiss the search party, thank them and tell them to report to their respective team leaders, then come back here.'

'Right, sir,' she said. Then she went out.

SIX

Angel was still in Miss Minter's little sitting room. He looked at his watch. It was twelve noon. He took the used brown envelope from his inside pocket and consulted it. He leaned back in the chair and rubbed the back of his neck and his chin and then closed his eyes. There was a lot to think about.

He stayed like that for several minutes, then he opened his mobile and scrolled down to a name and clicked on it.

A few seconds later, a voice said, 'Aye, Dr Mac speaking.'

Angel said, 'Now, you old haggis-eater, you've had a body there for almost forty-eight hours and I haven't heard a dickie bird from you. When were you going to ring me up and tell me about it?'

'Oh, it's you, Michael,' Mac said. 'You usually ring me up after I've had the corpse five minutes. Now you're waiting forty-eight hours. What's happening to you? You're slipping, Michael. You're getting relaxed, unconcerned and casual. What's happened to the fire in your belly?'

Angel grinned.

Mac said, 'As a matter of fact, it is on top of the pile to be typed out next.'

'Well, do you think you could nick it off the pile and give me the highlights?'

'Oh dear me,' the doctor said, pretending to be reluctant. 'The things I do for good Scottish–English relationships. Hold on . . . here we are. Well, there's nothing much. You already know most of it, I think. She died from a single shot to the cerebellum, lying posterior to the pons and medulla oblongata and inferior to the occipital lobes of the cerebral hemispheres, thus losing the maintenance of her posture and balance.'

'All right, Mac. You win. Let's have that in English.'

It was Mac's turn to crow. 'Well, she fell and hit her head on the corner of the piano stool, which would have stunned her and finished her off. She was dead by the time she hit the floor.'

There was a second's sombre silence, then Angel said, 'Anything else?'

'Well, what do you want? Her weight, height, operation scars, contents of stomach . . . ?'

'Contents of stomach. Yes,' Angel said with eyebrows raised. 'Anything there shouldn't have been?'

'Noo. Absolutely normal. Bloodstream, a trace of alcohol. Lungs, normal. Kidneys, normal.'

'Was there anything else *abnormal*?'

'Noo,' the doctor said.

Angel was disappointed. There was nothing helpful there. 'Well, thank you kindly, Mac,' he said.

'Anytime,' the doctor said with a smile on his lips.

Angel thoughtfully closed the phone, leaned back in the chair and squeezed the lobe of his ear between finger and thumb. A trace of alcohol in Joan Minter's bloodstream seemed perfectly reasonable considering she was at a party and she had a glass in her hand at the time she was shot. It was frustrating that there seemed to be such a dearth of clues on the body.

There was a knock at the door. It was Flora Carter.

'The search party has gone, sir,' she said. 'I had to organize transport back for them.'

'Right. Come in,' Angel said. 'Sit down.'

There was another knock on the door. It was Don Taylor.

When Angel saw him he stood up. 'Well, Don, what you got? Who has the blue specks with tails?'

'Nobody, sir. The hands of all four came up clean as a whistle.'

Angel slumped back in the chair. He looked down, closed his eyes and rubbed the back of his neck.

Flora said, 'Does that mean that they're no longer suspects?'

'No, not necessarily,' Taylor said. 'They could have been wearing gloves.'

'Are you sure you checked the right four?' Angel said.

Taylor sighed. 'Felix Lubrecki, Leo Altman, Erick Cartlett and Alexander Trott, sir,' he said.

Angel nodded. 'That's correct.'

Flora said, 'What I don't understand, sir, is how that butler chap, Trott, got so much lead, antimony and barium residue on his clothes. After all, he was standing at the other side of the room from the shooter, nearest the victim.'

Angel wrinkled his nose and said, 'Well, we are talking microscopic quantities, Flora. I expect the gunshot residues got onto Trott's clothes when he leaned over Miss Minter to see what help he could render.'

Taylor said, 'Well, sir, it doesn't look as if that test is going to help us in this case.'

Angel said, 'Well, so be it. There's nothing more we can do here. Don, I want you and your team to go post-haste to a robbery scene on Hemmsfield Road. See if you can find any forensic. The Control Room has the exact location and background. Trevor Crisp is there; liaise with him. I hope to get there soon myself.'

'Right, sir,' he said, and he went out.

Then Angel turned to DS Carter. 'Flora, provided we have their names and addresses and phone numbers, you can tell the guests and staff they can leave. Ask Mr Trott to see me before he goes.'

'Right, sir,' she said.

'And then come back here. I've got a job for you.'

'Right, sir,' she said again, and she went out.

A few moments later, there was a knock on the door. It was Trott.

Angel's eyebrows shot up. He noticed that the butler was no longer in a morning suit; instead he was wearing a smart brown suit, cream shirt with a patterned tie and brown shoes.

'Erm, you wanted to see me, Inspector?' Trott said.

'Come in, Mr Trott. Please sit down a moment.'

The butler did not look his usual composed self. He was running his hand over his hair and touching his chin and mouth.

'Yes,' Angel said. 'I need to know Miss Minter's next of kin. Can you tell me who that would be?'

Trott frowned, then said, 'I am not aware that she has any family living, Inspector, but I do know her solicitors are Pink and Cairncross on Eastgate. Mr Harry Cairncross used to visit her.'

Angel made a note. 'Thank you, Mr Trott. They probably know her next of kin and the contents of her will.'

'Was there anything else?'

'No. I don't think so.'

'I understand that you have finished your enquiries here,' Trott said. 'That pretty lady policewoman said that everybody should leave now, which made me suddenly realize that I am no longer in employment. For the first time in my life I am . . . I am out of work.'

'I shouldn't think you'd have much difficulty getting a new position.'

Trott shook his head. 'There's such a lot of unemployment and hardship about.'

'After all you didn't get the sack, did you?' Angel said. 'And I trust you have some savings to tide you over for a week or two while you find something.'

'Well, I have, of course. And I could go and stay with my sister in Southport for a while. But I would rather stay here. I have my own room and all my things are here. Do you think that would be possible?'

'It's not for me to say, Mr Trott. But I shouldn't think anybody would have any objection if you stayed for a few days. Give my "pretty sergeant" your new address, whatever you decide.'

'Yes, Inspector. I will. And thank you. You've cheered me up.'

Angel smiled.

'There's something else, Inspector. Well, two things, really. Have you found out who murdered Miss Minter?'

'No, Mr Trott. But we will.'

Trott smiled. 'Good. Your name came to me the other day. Inspector Angel. You're a celebrity, aren't you? You're the policeman who *always* gets his man, like the Mounties. I've read about you in a magazine somewhere. And there are so many murders that are never solved, but you've always managed to solve your cases and catch the murderer, haven't you?'

Angel rubbed his chin, blew out a long breath and said, 'Well, I have up to now.' Then he quickly added, 'What was the other thing?'

Trott was still smiling. 'Oh yes,' he said, then he frowned. 'Miss Bell, Miss Minter's secretary and the caterers, Mr and Mrs Jones, have not been paid. I somehow feel responsible . . .'

Angel said, 'I should recommend them to contact Miss Minter's solicitors.'

Trott smiled. 'Yes, of course,' he said.

He stood up and turned towards the door. 'Now why didn't I think of that?' he added. 'Thank you, Inspector. Goodbye.'

As he went out, Flora Carter came in.

'Everybody seems pleased except the caterers, sir,' she said.

'They'll be worried about being paid,' Angel said. Then he added, 'Flora, I want you to call on Mrs Vera Sellars. She lives at number 24 on this road. That's the woman who had her handbag stolen recently. Get a list of everything that was in it. *Everything*. You understand?'

'Right, sir.'

'I'm going to Hemmsfield junction.'

It was two o'clock when Angel arrived at the road junction where the Slater Security van had crashed and been robbed. The area was taped off and No Entry signs and diversion signs were all round the locale.

A uniformed constable recognized Angel in the BMW. He saluted him, lifted the tape and waved him underneath. Angel saw Crisp's car and parked next to it. As he got out he saw that Crisp was in the car with two men in Slater Security livery.

The SOCO van was parked ten yards further away alongside the wreck, and DS Taylor and a detective constable were in their white disposable paper suits, carefully picking their way through the back of the wrecked blue and white van.

Another SOCO was in the cab of the Volkswagen with a flask of aluminium powder and a brush, looking for fingerprints.

Angel went up to DS Crisp's car and opened the door.

Crisp made the introductions, then Angel looked at Crisp and said, 'Can I have a word, Trevor?' Then he left the car door open and walked a few paces away.

Crisp got out, closed the car door and went up to him.

Angel said, 'Did they see any of the gang's faces?'

'No, sir. There were four in the gang, all wearing black or navy-blue balaclavas, and three of them — they'd be in their twenties and thirties — were wearing jeans, woollen jumpers and trainers. The fourth, who seemed to be the gang leader, had very broad shoulders and was about forty. He was the one who rammed the van with the car. He was wearing protective pads round his legs and arms over a dark suit, and he had a safety helmet over the balaclava.'

Angel rubbed his temple. 'Were there any firearms?'

‘Yes, sir. The driver who rammed them. He had a small, sort of blue-coloured handgun.’

Angel shook his head and wiped over his face with his hand. ‘Too many guns around the place. What do they know about their getaway?’

‘They said that the four men made their escape in a blue Ford Mondeo, sir. They went north towards Leeds. They didn’t get the licence number.’

‘It would have been a false number plate, anyway,’ Angel said. ‘Did they get away with a lot?’

‘Two hundred and twenty thousand, sir.’

His eyes opened wide. ‘It’s a lot of money,’ he said, shaking his head.

‘Another thing, sir. The notes were all dirty or torn notes on their way to the Bank of England to be destroyed.’

‘Did Slater’s men see anything helpful at all? You know, a tattoo, a wristwatch, that sort of thing?’

‘They said not, sir,’ Crisp said. ‘This gang weren’t amateurs. They seem to have left the job absolutely clean.’

Angel’s eyes flashed. The muscles round his jaw tightened. ‘Nobody can deliberately drive a car into a van at speed, blow open the door of the safe, take away all that dosh and not leave *something* behind.’

‘They left three pickaxes, sir.’

‘Yeah, I mean more than that. I’m hopeful that Don Taylor will find something . . . a print or something. All right, Trevor. Carry on, but press them on anything they might have seen or heard of the robbers.’

‘I will, sir,’ Crisp said, and he returned to the two Slater Security men in his car.

Angel walked up to the vehicle wreck. ‘Is Don Taylor there?’

The tall slim figure wreathed in white came out of the innermost part of the van. ‘Yes, sir?’ he said.

‘How you doing, Don?’

He pulled down his mask and said, ‘Found a cigarette end, sir. The brand is “Adelaide”. Never heard of it. No prints on it. Looks like all the gang were wearing gloves, and that that discipline was maintained throughout.'

Angel's face creased. 'Can we get any DNA from it?'

'Yes, sir.'

'That would be great, if they're on record,' Angel said, rubbing his chin. Then his forehead wrinkled. 'Just a minute,' he said, and he walked back to Crisp's car, opened the door, peered in and said, 'Excuse me, chaps.' He looked at the two Slater Security men and said, 'Do either of you smoke?'

'No,' came the reply in unison.

He nodded, closed the car door, came back to Taylor and said, 'It's not from either of them.'

Taylor smiled. 'Great stuff, sir. We'll get it off to the lab today.'

'Find anything else, Don?'

'We've been over the three pickaxes they used to claw their way into the back of the van, but there are no prints or anything useful on them.'

'Right. I'll take them with me. Get one of your lads to put them in my boot, will you?'

'Yes, sir.'

'Anything else?'

'I've found part of the remains of the detonator, sir. A handmade job. Quite primitive but it works. Made from a three-inch length of steel wool, two matches, six inches of Sellotape, several yards of twin-core electric cable and a little nine-volt battery. A kid of ten could make it. And so efficient. The detonation is so quick that the blast of the dynamite blows out the flame of the two matches before they are burnt up.'

Angel blinked several times. 'Interesting from the modus operandi point of view, Don,' he said, 'but there's nothing forensic we can learn from that, is there?'

Taylor didn't reply quickly. He scratched his head, then said, 'It helps to measure the size of the explosion, sir.'

'True. And the mentality of the villains.'

'It's that sort of info you'd get from a spell in prison.'

Angel nodded his agreement. 'I reckon it would cost about two snorts of cocaine.'

'The currency used to be cigarettes.'

'Have you found anything else?'

'No, sir, but we're not quite finished.'

'Have you been over the Volkswagen?'

'There's a man looking for prints now, sir. There are no sweet papers, no lager cans, no fag ends, nothing.'

'Leave it with you, then.'

Taylor turned back to the wreck.

Angel walked down the line to Crisp's car and opened the door again. He looked at the older of the two Slater's men. 'Excuse me again, gentlemen. Is your office sending some transport to get you two home?'

'Yes, thank you,' he said. 'Our boss is coming down; so is a man to sort out the insurance.'

Angel nodded. 'Right.' Then he turned back to Crisp. 'I'm going back to the station, Trevor. I'll have to get this wreck moved before it's dark.'

It was four o'clock.

There was a knock on Angel's office door.

Angel was seated at his desk. 'Yes? Come in,' he said.

It was Ahmed. 'Ah yes,' Angel said. 'There are three pickaxes in the boot of my car. Take them down to SOCO.' He reached into his pocket and gave Ahmed his car key. 'You'll need that. Get a photographer to take a picture of all three together. I want the "Stronghold" brand label round the handle of each pickaxe to be readable on at least one of them. Then put the pic online. All right?'

'Right, sir.'

Ahmed went out.

Angel picked up the phone and dialled a two-digit number. It was an internal call to Norman Mallin, the sergeant responsible for station transport. He instructed him to organize the immediate recovery of the two crashed vehicles out at Hemmsfield.

He then rang Simon Bennett, chief news reporter at the *Bromersley Chronicle.*

'I've got a story for you,' Angel said. 'You will be the first to hear it. It's about the robbery of a Slater Security van carrying—'

'Oh, *that,*' Bennett said. '*That's* what that road blockage out at Hemmsfield is all about, isn't it, Michael? I heard they got away with two hundred and twenty thousand pounds.'

Angel licked his lips. His grip on the phone tightened. He hadn't reckoned on Bennett knowing so much. He recovered quickly and said, 'That's right, and I want you to do me a little favour.'

Bennett said, 'Of course, Michael. If I can, I will. What is it?'

'I want you to use a photograph of the three pickaxes used in the crime. And I want a mention that if anybody remembers selling them recently, to get in touch with the police. I can send you the photograph online.'

'Not a very interesting photograph, three pickaxes, Michael,' Bennett said.

'No, but it might give us a lead to the gang,' Angel said. 'You'd be doing a great public service, Simon, particularly if the photograph pulled in information that led to the arrest of the armed robbers.'

There was a short silence. Angel reckoned he could hear Bennett thinking.

'Yes, all right, Michael,' the reporter said.

So Angel told him all about the robbery, carefully avoiding the finding of the cigarette butt. Bennett asked a couple of questions for clarification, which Angel answered quickly, and the call was ended.

Angel reached into his desk drawer, took out the local telephone directory. He turned to the pages with names beginning with P. He scanned down the columns and found the name Pink and Cairncross, Solicitors, Eastgate, Bromersley. He tapped in their number and was soon speaking to Mr Harry Cairncross.

'I understand you are the solicitor of the late Miss Joan Minter?' Angel said.

'That is correct, Inspector. It is not very long since I drew up the will.'

'Mr Cairncross, can you tell me who the executors of Miss Minter's estate are?'

'We are, Inspector. There are no known relatives alive of Miss Minter.'

'And who is the sole or main beneficiary?'

'Her butler, Alexander Trott,' Cairncross said.

Angel blinked rapidly, then stared ahead open-mouthed at nothing in particular.

'Hello. Are you still there, Inspector?' Cairncross said.

Angel shook his head in an effort to think clearly. 'Yes. Yes, I'm here, Mr Cairncross. Thank you. Thank you very much. Goodbye.'

He slowly replaced the phone. He was surprised at the news.

Armed with this new information on Trott, he considered all the other facts he had on him, then dismissed the subject. He then took out the old envelope from his inside pocket to check off all the jobs he had to do. He was peering down at it and striking his ballpoint through the tasks he had already attended to when there was a knock at the door.

It was Ahmed.

'What do you want, lad?'

The young policeman rushed in breathless, his eyes sparkling, his face red. 'Thought you'd like to know, sir. I was in the Control Room when it came in. A triple nine. There's a car just seen on fire in Cheapo's car park. The sergeant's advised the fire brigade.'

Angel frowned. 'So what?' he said. 'It happens now and then. Kids steal a car and drive round till they're bored out of their drugged-up little minds, then they carve up the upholstery for laughs, smash all the headlights for fun and set it on fire for a lark. Then they run off and watch it burn from a safe distance and see how law-abiding citizens cope with it. It makes a change from sticking a steak knife in another young man's stomach.'

Ahmed's eyes remained bright. 'Ah, yes, sir,' the young man said, 'but this was a nearly new blue Ford Mondeo. Could be the stolen one used in the robbery of the Slater Security van.'

Angel pulled his head back. His eyes grew big and unblinking. Then he said, 'Ah, I see. Well spotted, Ahmed.' He leaped up, sending the swivel chair backwards. It hit the wall with a bang. He reached out for his hat and coat and was gone.

SEVEN

It was 8.28 a.m. on Wednesday, 5 November, Fireworks Day.

Angel walked down the corridor, passed the CID office and entered his office.

Ahmed appeared from nowhere, knocked on the door and came in waving a newspaper around.

'Good morning, sir,' he said. 'It's full of stuff about Joan Minter and the investigation.'

Angel looked up. He was eager to read it, but there were important things that had priority. 'Thank you, Ahmed,' he said, 'But I must go out to Cheapo's and see what that wreck can tell us.' He quickly glanced through a pile of envelopes that had been added since the previous afternoon, looked round the office, then made for the door.

'Shall I leave it here, sir,' Ahmed said, putting it on his desk, 'and pick it up later?'

'Yes. Thank you. Do that. Must go,' Angel said from the door. 'By the way, your paper from yesterday is in the middle drawer of my desk. Help yourself to it.'

'Thank you, sir.'

Angel spent most of the remainder of the morning with DS Taylor. Together they looked through the burnt-out wreck of the Ford Mondeo that had featured so prominently in the robbery of the Slater Security van. Angel had been hopeful of finding something that would help identify one of the gang of robbers, but there was nothing. If there had been any prints, they had disappeared in the heat of the fire.

They gave up the search at about twelve noon and Angel returned to his office, where he found on his desk the morning paper that Ahmed had left, as well as three pickaxes and six photographs of them.

He picked up the paper and saw the front-page story was still about the murder of Joan Minter. It was headed by an ancient picture of her playing the female lead in *Romeo and Juliet*. He quickly read it, then turned the page to find lots of detail about the investigation of the case: some was accurate some was intelligent guesswork.

However, contained in the text he noticed the words, 'The results of the gunshot residue tests arrived by police courier,' which made him think. He blinked, lowered the paper and looked straight ahead at nothing in particular. He rubbed his chin. How would a reporter *know* that the results of the tests arrived by police courier? How does anybody except the people who send and receive them know? When a police courier arrives, he doesn't broadcast what he is delivering. He just hands it over and gets a signature for it. He probably has no idea what's in the envelope or package. It might be confidential, wanted urgently, highly valuable or evidence of vital importance in determining someone's guilt or innocence. He might realize that it could be some or all those factors, but he wouldn't *know*.

He toyed with the puzzle for a few moments, then he turned back the newspaper page to the front, noted that it was the *Daily Yorkshireman* and folded it neatly and put it on one side to be returned to Ahmed.

He then tapped a number into his phone to summon DC Scrivens.

'Come in, Ted,' Angel said. 'Sit down a minute.'

Scrivens stared at the pickaxes on the desk in front of him, then sat down.

Angel said, 'What are you busy with?'

'A complaint about kids making a nuisance of themselves, sir,' Scrivens said. 'Letting off bangers outside an old people's home. Usual Guy Fawkes troubles.'

Angel shook his head. 'Annoying little monkeys. Can you pass that on to somebody else?'

'Yes, sir.'

'You'll have heard about this robbery out at Hemmsfield?' Angel said. 'I want you to take one of these pickaxes and call on all the hardware shops, garden shops, garden centres, builders' supplies merchants . . . the sort of outlets that might have sold them. Ask the sales staff if they can recall selling *three* of these to the *same* customer during the past few days. That has got to be unusual. They might even have CCTV of the customer if we are lucky. Anyway, try to get a description of the person who bought them. All right?'

'Right, sir,' Scrivens said. He stood up.

The phone began to ring.

Angel looked at it, handed Scrivens a pickaxe, then one of the photographs. 'Here. Take one of these. It's a photograph of all three pickaxes.'

The phone seemed insistent.

'I'd better answer it,' Angel said. 'Hang on a minute.'

'Right, sir.'

He picked up the phone. 'Angel,' he said.

It was Superintendent Harker. '*There* you are,' he said with a sniff. 'Just had a triple nine. A woman has returned to her house and found her husband dead on the floor of the kitchen. Her name is Fairclough, address, 33 Melvinia Crescent. I've advised SOCO.'

Angel's pulse raced. 'Right, sir,' he said, 'I'll get straight onto—'

But Harker had gone.

Angel replaced the phone, looked up and saw Scrivens. 'Right, Ted. Erm . . . if you manage to strike lucky, ring me on my mobile.'

'Right, sir,' Scrivens said, and he made for the door.

'Oh, Ted,' Angel said. 'Tell Ahmed I want him.'

'Right, sir,' he said, and he went out.

Angel reached out for the phone again. He tapped in an internal number.

It was soon answered. 'Control Room. Sergeant Clifton.'

There was a knock at the door. It was Ahmed. Angel waved him in.

'Bernie,' Angel said into the phone. 'I need two PCs to attend at 33 Melvinia Crescent.'

'Right, sir, I'll see to it.'

'Thank you.' He replaced the phone. He looked up at Ahmed and said, 'Got to go to 33 Melvinia Crescent. Find Flora Carter and ask her to meet me there ASAP.'

'Right, sir,' Ahmed said, and he went out.

Angel reached out for his coat and hat.

Angel reached 33 Melvinia Crescent in a few minutes. It was one of around forty red-brick semi-detached houses built in the thirties in a leafy part of Bromersley, where hedgehogs and squirrels could still occasionally be seen. Up the short concrete drive was SOCO's white van.

He parked the BMW in the road, got out, went up to the front door and banged hard on it. At the same moment, he heard footsteps running up behind him. He turned to see that it was DS Carter. She arrived slightly out of breath. She smiled at him.

'Made it,' she said. 'Just got back from seeing Mrs Sellars, sir . . . getting that list of the contents of her handbag.'

'Oh yes. I'll see to that later,' he said. 'This is reported as a murder case.'

She bit her bottom lip and said, 'Yes, sir. Ahmed told me.'

A detective constable in a white disposable suit opened the door.

'Is DS Taylor there?' Angel said.

'I'll get him, sir,' the man said, and he turned away.

Taylor must have heard his name because he came forward.

'Ah, Don,' Angel said. 'We can't come in. We're not kitted out.'

'I'll come out, sir,' Taylor said. He stepped out onto the step and closed the door.

'What you got, then?' Angel said.

Taylor ran a hand across his face. 'Man about forty, understand he lived here with his wife. Found, by her, in a pool of blood, on the kitchen floor. Shot in the head. He's called Ian Fairclough. Hasn't been dead long.'

'How long?'

'The body is not really cold and there are no signs of rigor mortis, sir.'

Angel knew that as a general rule, rigor mortis doesn't set in for the first three hours after death unless the person had beforehand been engaged in excessive physical exertion. Therefore, it seemed that as it was 1 p.m. now, the victim had died sometime after 10 a.m. that morning.

Angel nodded. 'You said his wife found him?' he said.

'Yes, sir. She had been out at work, came in today at about half past twelve. She said she promptly dialled 999.'

Angel frowned. 'Any sign of the murder weapon?'

'No, sir.'

'What about the wife?'

'Naturally, very distraught. She said that she didn't see anybody, and that she knows nothing. She says that this is a complete mystery to her.'

'Where is she now?'

'Being comforted by a neighbour at number 28.' He pointed to a house across the road behind Angel. 'That one, sir.'

'Right. Have you informed Dr Mac?'

'He's on his way, sir.'

'How long will it take you to clear the scene of crime?'

'About an hour, I should think.'

Angel looked at his watch. 'See you then, Don.'

Taylor went inside and closed the door.

Angel turned right round and looked at all the houses he could see. It was practically the entire estate, because the road curved round. Then he turned to Carter and said, 'Look how many windows we can see from this point, Flora. Must be several hundred. If we can see them, they can see us. I want to know if anybody saw a visitor to this house this morning. You take the odd numbers and I'll take the even numbers. Call on every house that can see this path and this front door.'

'Right, sir,' she said.

'Meet me at number 28,' he said. He clenched his jaw and added, 'I shall *have* to interview the murdered man's wife. I'll be there when I have done.'

He went down to the BMW, unlocked it and took out a clipboard holding a paper pad and set off to the house furthest away on his side. It was number 12. There was no reply there nor at some of the other houses and he assumed they were out at work. He kept a note of those who didn't respond. The householders that he did manage to speak to said that they hadn't noticed anybody strange on the crescent that morning. Having called on all the other even-numbered houses, he took a deep breath and knocked on the door of number 28. A woman opened it.

'Good morning,' he said. 'I'm DI Angel from Bromersley Police. Here's my ID.'

'That's all right, dear. We've been expecting you. You'll be wanting to see Susan. Come on in. She's resting in the front room.'

Angel went inside and closed the door. He was in the kitchen. He glanced round. It was spotless.

'Thank you,' he said. 'May I have your name?'

She smiled at him. 'Isabel. But everybody calls me Belle. What's your name again, dear?'

'Inspector Angel, miss.'

She gave him another big smile.

She was far from pretty, but a dimple appeared in her cheek when she smiled.

'It's Mrs, actually,' she said. 'Mrs Beasley. There hasn't been a Mr Beasley for twelve years now.'

Angel said, 'Oh, I'm so sorry.'

'I'm not,' she said with a grin. 'Leaving me was the only good thing he ever did for me. This way.' She turned to go.

Angel rubbed his chin. 'Just a minute, Mrs Beasley.'

She turned back.

He said, 'Did you see anybody across at Mrs Fairclough's anytime this morning?'

'No, Inspector, I would have told you. We don't like strangers on Melvinia Crescent. Do you want to see Susan Fairclough?'

He nodded. 'I just wanted to be sure.'

She opened the door and Angel followed her into a plain but comfortable little room with a three-piece suite, coffee table and a gas fire.

A small, slim woman of around forty was relaxing on the settee. When Angel appeared she stood up, holding one arm by the elbow. She glanced at him, then looked down at the floor, then looked up at him again, then at Mrs Beasley, then at the door.

'I'm sorry, Mrs Fairclough. I didn't mean to disturb you.'

'That's all right,' she said in a small voice. 'I can't lounge about here all the time.'

Mrs Beasley beamed and in a loud voice said, 'You can stay here as long as you like, Susan. You know that.'

Mrs Fairclough looked across at her and smiled weakly.

'I'm DI Angel,' he said. 'I'd like to ask you a few questions.'

'Yes. Of course. I suppose you want a statement?'

'No. No. Nothing formal at this stage,' he said.

He turned back, looked at Mrs Beasley and nodded.

She blinked, wriggled both of her shoulders and then said, 'I'd better get on with my work. I've the washing to do.' She turned towards the door.

Angel said, 'Mrs Beasley, I'm expecting my sergeant. Send her in when she arrives, would you?'

'Righto,' she said as she closed the door.

He turned back to Susan Fairclough. 'Now then, why don't you sit down?' he said.

She turned, adjusted a cushion and sat on the edge of the settee.

'Is that better?' he said. 'Why not sit further back?'

She shuffled a little.

Angel rubbed his chin. 'Now then, Mrs Fairclough, have you any idea who would want to harm your husband?'

'None whatsoever,' she said. 'He was a perfectly lovely man.'

'Was he in employment?'

'Oh yes. He worked for the Indemnity and Life Insurance Company of London. It's a big firm. He'd been there all his working life.'

'What exactly did he do?'

'He helped people with their insurance claims and sold them policies.'

'And was he happy doing that?'

'Very. I've met the chairman of the company. He seemed to think the world of him.

'Insurance is all Ian knows anything about. We haven't any close friends and we don't go out much. We're not interested in socializing. I can't believe what's happened. It doesn't make any sense.'

He nodded.

'Besides all that, Inspector,' she said, 'several other strange things happened at my house today.'

Angel blinked. 'Oh? Like what?' he said.

The room door suddenly opened.

His fists clenched as he turned round to see what was happening.

Mrs Beasley put her head round the door. ''Scuse me,' she said, 'but your sergeant is here, Inspector.'

The door opened wider and Flora Carter came in.

'Thank you, Mrs Beasley,' Angel said.

She closed the door.

Flora looked round as she unbuttoned her coat.

Angel was pleased to see her. He was eager to know if any of the householders she had called on had seen a stranger anywhere near number 33 that morning. Her eyes met his. He looked at her and raised his eyebrows.

She shook her head.

The muscles round his mouth tightened and he frowned. Then he brought Flora up to scratch with what he had already learned and asked her to keep a note of what was said. Flora then settled in the other easy chair with her notebook and pen at the ready.

Angel said, 'Now, Mrs Fairclough, sorry about that . . . you were saying that several strange things happened at your house today.'

'Yes. Firstly my dear husband should have been in London today. He left by train for London yesterday and was supposed to be returning late on Friday. It was to do with his work. He had these sales meetings about twice a year.'

'So today he should have been at the head office of the Indemnity and Life Insurance Company in London?'

'Yes,' Mrs Fairclough said. 'And if there had been a change of plan, I am surprised that he didn't phone me.'

Angel nodded. He glanced at Flora Carter to see that she was writing this down. Then he looked back at Mrs Fairclough and said, 'What else struck you as strange?'

'Well,' she said, 'in the entrance hall of my house is an olive-green vacuum cleaner. It was the first thing I saw when I came in at lunchtime. I think it is brand new. Still has some wrappings on it. Now, I don't know whose it is. It's certainly not ours. I wouldn't have chosen that colour anyway. We don't need it. We don't want it. I'm certain Ian wouldn't have bought it. It would be right out of character. He doesn't concern himself with things like vacuum cleaners. If we had needed one, we would have talked about it, budgeted for it and he would have probably left it to me to decide on the colour, the model and the price and so on. I hope I'm not going to get a bill for it from somebody.'

Angel rubbed his chin lightly. 'What else was strange?' he said.

'Well, the fridge door was left wide open. Everybody knows not to leave a fridge door open, don't they? Ian would not have left it open like that. The murderer must have done that, but why?'

'Is there anything missing from there?'

'I really don't know. I didn't . . . I couldn't . . . I just closed it.'

'Is there anything missing from the house? Have you been robbed of anything?'

'I don't know. I didn't bother to . . .' Her voice trailed away.

'I understand. That's all right, Mrs Fairclough. We've nearly finished for now. Where were you this morning? Were you out?'

'I am a schoolteacher. Full-time. I teach at the school at the end of this road, Wakefield Road Middle School. I usually come home at lunchtime and sometimes have a quick, light lunch with Ian, if he isn't travelling far away. I should have phoned the headmistress and told her why I'm not there. Oh dear.'

'My sergeant here will do that for you. Won't you, Flora?'

'Of course,' she said, producing her mobile.

Mrs Fairclough shook her head. 'No. No. Thank you,' she said. 'I must do it myself. You said we were almost finished.'

'And so we are, for now, Mrs Fairclough,' Angel said. 'There's just one matter I'd like you to clear up, if you can. You said that your husband left yesterday for London by train: well, where did he spend last night?'

She closed her eyes a few seconds to think about the answer, then she said, 'The arrangements were that he was going to London by train on Tuesday — yesterday — and would be returning late Thursday about half past nine. I don't know where he was staying in London, he didn't say. But I could always get in touch with him on his mobile. I don't know where he stayed last night, nor do I know why he came home early.'

'Never mind, Mrs Fairclough. We will try and find the answers. Thank you very much, for now.'

EIGHT

It was after 2 p.m. when Angel and Flora Carter made their way across the road to 33 Melvinia Crescent.

DS Taylor opened the door to them. 'Good timing, sir,' he said. 'We've about finished here.'

They went inside the entrance hall and closed the door. Angel noticed the green vacuum cleaner. It was as Susan Fairclough had said: still partly wrapped in polythene. It was obviously unused and new.

'It seems that it was brought to the house and left here by the murderer, Don, although I don't know why,' Angel said. 'You'd better check it first of all for explosives.'

Taylor blinked. His face straightened. 'Explosives, sir?' he said.

Angel's shoulders went up, he held out his hands palms upwards and said, 'Or hidden transmitter. I can't think of any sensible reason for it to be here. But I also want you to see if there are any prints or any other forensics that may lead to indicating who has handled it in the last twenty-four hours or so.'

Taylor nodded.

'Now, where's the body?' Angel said.

'In the kitchen, sir. Through there. Dr Mac's still working on it.'

The little Glaswegian heard them and said, 'Nay. I've finished here noo, Michael. I just want the nod from ye.' He had closed his bag and was getting to his feet.

'I'll just have a look, Mac . . . and then you can have it.'

Angel squatted down and looked closely at the dead man. Flora blinked rapidly several times. She had her bottom lip between her teeth as she leaned forward. In her own mind, she was not certain how much of the body and the crime scene she wanted to see.

The body was lying on the white and black kitchen floor tiles. It was of a clean-shaven, fresh-faced man in a dark-grey suit, with collar, tie and polished black leather shoes. The eyes were open and seemed to stare at the kitchen wall. The head had a black hole at the temple and there was dried blood over the cheek and on the floor tiles.

After a few moments, Angel stood up.

Flora shook her head, put a hand on her chest and swallowed uncomfortably. 'Why didn't somebody close his eyes?' she muttered.

Dr Mac looked at Angel and said, 'The fair citizens of Bromersley are keeping you busy, I see.'

'*Too* busy, I'd say,' Angel said. 'What have you got, then, Mac?'

The doctor wrinkled his nose and said, 'Male, about forty years. Shot once in the temple at close range. Died instantly, sometime between 9.30 and 11.30 this morning.'

Angel rubbed the back of his neck and said, 'Hmmm. Thank you, Mac. You can take him as soon as you like.'

'Right,' he said. He turned away and dug into his pocket for his mobile.

Angel went out into the hall looking for Taylor. He was taking prints off the vacuum cleaner.

Taylor looked up at him and said, 'There aren't any explosives present in this cleaner, sir. And there isn't a bug that I recognize planted on it.'

Angel nodded and said, 'Well, what is the point of the damned thing?'

Taylor grinned. 'Who knows?'

'Who knows indeed,' Angel said. 'Where is the bullet case, Don?'

'Haven't come across it, sir.'

Angel's eyes flashed. 'Well, there's bound to be one. Unless we have an intellectual murderer who took it with him to confuse us. And if he did, it'll be the first time I've ever known it happen. They're usually in an understandable hurry to get as far away from the scene of the crime as possible.'

He looked round the kitchen. There was a tall fridge next to the kitchen sink. He called out to Taylor in the hall. 'This the only fridge in the house?'

'Yes, sir. Did you expect more than one?'

'No. Mrs Fairclough said the fridge door was wide open when she came in. I wondered why.'

Taylor came into the kitchen, opened the fridge door, quickly looked inside, then closed it. 'Is it significant, sir?'

Angel shrugged. 'I don't know. But it would be good to have an explanation, wouldn't it?'

'Someone wanted to get something out of it in a hurry?' Taylor said.

'Could be.'

Flora said, 'Someone wanted to get something out of it in a hurry who didn't care about the condition of the rest of the fridge's contents.'

'Absolutely,' Angel said. 'That's likely to be the intruder or murderer rather than the victim.'

Taylor said, 'But the murderer's prints weren't on the fridge door handle, only smudges.'

Angel said, 'Mrs Fairclough told me she came into the house and found it wide open, so she closed it. It is unfortunate, but there we are. That's what she says happened. So if it had had any fingerprints they would have been hers.'

'So it doesn't matter then, sir, does it?' Taylor said.

Angel gritted his teeth and ran a hand through his hair. 'Of course it matters. The existence of Susan Fairclough's clear fingerprints on the fridge door would have proven that she was telling the truth, even though it was in itself trivial and apparently inconsequential. You know, Don, that some witnesses sometimes lie. So it would have been nice, as an example, to have confirmation that this witness, in this instance, told the truth.'

Taylor gave a little shrug, then returned to the hall to carry on with the vacuum cleaner.

Angel, followed by Flora, went into the living room. It was neat and presentable. He saw a delicately decorated and chased three-piece silver tea set on the sideboard. He picked up the teapot, turned it over and looked for the silver marks. He saw a lion passant, a leopard's head, a king's head and the letter 'b'. His eyebrows shot up. 'Phew!' he said as he replaced it. 'Georgian. A couple of grand at least, and on open display.'

Flora said, 'The murderer wasn't a thief, then, sir?'

He scratched his head. 'Well, certainly not this morning,' he said.

'Maybe he just didn't notice it?'

'Mebbe. Let's just have a quick look upstairs.'

They passed Taylor in the hall and mounted the stairs.

Everything was well looked after, clean and tidy. The largest bedroom at the front had a conventional dressing table situated in front of the window. He saw a gilt metal box between a hairbrush and a hand mirror on a cut-glass tray. He opened the box and saw several rings and earrings. He picked up the largest ring, which had an impressive baguette-cut green stone in the middle and twelve old cut diamonds around it. He showed it to the sergeant.

'If that's a real emerald, Flora — and I think it probably is — there's another couple of grand. Could be more.'

She looked at it and smiled. 'I wouldn't mind a ring like that, sir.'

'Don't marry a copper, then,' he said.

She smiled at him.

He replaced the ring and closed the gilt box.

She said, 'More evidence that the killer wasn't a thief, sir?'

'Well, I don't know, Flora. He certainly didn't seem to have stealing in mind while he was here this morning.'

They went downstairs. Taylor was still in the hall by the vacuum cleaner. 'There are no fresh prints on it, sir,' he said.

'Right, Don,' Angel said, wrinkling his nose. 'Another dead end.'

There was suddenly a shout from the kitchen. It was Dr Mac. 'I've found it, Michael. I've found it.'

Angel, Taylor and Flora dashed out of the hall to the kitchen.

Dr Mac pointed to the tile floor at a small, shiny brass bullet case. 'I was just straightening him up before rigor mortis sets in, and I moved a leg and that rolled out from underneath his trews.'

'Aaah!' Angel said, patting Mac lightly on the back. 'We are going to need that for Ballistics.'

Taylor crouched down and got hold of the bullet case by inserting his pen into it and then turning it upright.

'What calibre is it, Don?' Angel said.

'Looks like a .32 ACP, sir,' Taylor said. 'I'll just check it for prints.' He rushed off to find his brush and tin of aluminium powder.

Flora Carter turned to Angel and said, 'What's ACP stand for, sir?'

'Automatic Colt Pistol,' Angel said. 'It's an old classification. Today it is usually used simply to describe a cartridge with straight sides as opposed to cartridges with tapering sides.'

She nodded.

'Flora,' he said, 'will you go across the road and see if Mrs Fairclough is up to coming back here? I'd like to settle one or two things. Don't push her if she's not up to it.'

'Right, sir,' she said, and off she went.

Angel went back into the entrance hall. He was looking for Taylor. He saw him at the sitting-room window peering closely at the bullet case on the end of his pen. He was rotating it, looking for fingerprints with an 8x loupe in his eye.

'Ah, Don,' Angel said. 'I was wondering how the murderer gained access to the house. Were there any signs of a break-in?'

'No, sir,' Taylor said. 'The doors and windows were all sound.'

Angel nodded. He wrinkled his nose. He wasn't pleased.

'There are no prints on this bullet case, sir,' Taylor said, taking it off his pen and wiping off the silver-coloured aluminium powder he had lightly dusted onto it.

Angel's lips tightened. He shook his head. 'Crooks are getting too smart these days.'

Taylor said, 'There are lots of prints on the vacuum cleaner, but no recent ones.'

Angel wrinkled his nose again. He rubbed his chin. 'I assume that it was sold or stolen from a retail business of some sort,' he said. 'An electrical shop, a warehouse or the like. If we could find out . . . Is there a price ticket or label on it that would give us an indication of where it came from?'

'No, sir, nothing.'

'Huh,' he grunted. 'There *wouldn't* be. Right, Don, thank you.'

Then Angel turned away. He wasn't pleased.

His muscles strained against the skin. His pulse pounded in his ears. He inhaled deeply through his nose then exhaled through his mouth.

Nothing was easy these days. However, it was when cases were difficult that he excelled. He had a record to maintain.

He dived into his pocket and pulled out his mobile. He scrolled down to a name and clicked on it. It was to DS Crisp. It was ringing out. After a while it went to voicemail. At that, Angel's face went scarlet. His eyes stuck out like bilberries on stalks. '*Ring me back*,' he said. '*And it had better be soon!*' He closed the phone and stuffed it into his pocket.

He breathed deeply several times then looked around.

Two men came in with a stretcher on wheels. They went out a few minutes later with Ian Fairclough's body on it under a white plastic sheet.

When they had gone, Doctor Mac appeared in the hall. He had discarded the whites and wellington boots. He was wearing his overcoat and carrying his bag.

'Cheerio, Michael,' he said. 'I'll send you the PM in a couple of days.'

Angel waved. He smiled and said, 'Earlier if possible, Mac.'

The white-haired man's eyes narrowed and he shook his head as he went out into the hall. He knew that a couple of days was a very quick turnaround for any pathologist in this situation. He had already told Angel the time and cause of death. He then realized that he was being teased. He quickly turned and said, 'The impossible will take a week, Michael, and costs twice the price.'

Angel grinned.

The front door closed.

Taylor came up to him.

'We're done here, sir. We've just to pack up. I didn't find anything useful on the body, nor the vacuum cleaner.'

Angel had already realized that. 'If it isn't there, it isn't there.'

'When I get back I'll see Control and make sure the house is guarded overnight, if you like.'

'Thank you, Don.'

Angel turned away to the front window. He took out the old envelope from his pocket, looked at his notes and checked down the list.

Taylor and his team began to take their packs and equipment out to the van via the front door.

Angel suddenly looked up and said, 'Anybody seen a telephone directory?'

One of the constables of SOCO's team came forward. 'I've seen one in here,' he said, indicating the sideboard drawer. He pulled it open and handed it to Angel.

'Thank you, lad,' Angel said, and he scrambled through the pages. He soon found the number he was looking for, and tapped it into his mobile.

A few seconds later a woman answered. 'Wakefield Road Middle School.'

'This is DI Angel of Bromersley Police. Can I speak to the headmaster or headmistress, please?'

'I am the headmistress, Marjorie Thompson,' she said. 'Oh dear, I suppose it's about poor Susan Fairclough.'

'I'm afraid it is,' he said. 'I am the investigating officer looking into her husband's death. Can you please tell me if she was at school this morning?'

'Of course. She was in school all morning. She took her own class this morning until break and then she took 2B until lunchtime.'

'What time do you call lunchtime, Mrs Thompson?'

'We break for lunch at 12.30. May I say that Mrs Fairclough is a wonderful and most valuable teacher, much cared for by the staff here — and the pupils. And that her husband was a lovely man and that they were very close and highly respected. They lived only for each other.'

'Thank you very much for that, Mrs Thompson. Goodbye.'

He cancelled the call and the mobile immediately began to ring.

He saw it was Crisp calling.

Angel breathed in quickly, his stomach clenched tight and his hand squeezed the phone. He put the phone to his ear and pressed the button.

'Good afternoon, sir,' Crisp said.

Through clenched teeth, Angel said, 'Where the hell have you been?'

'I've been here in the station all afternoon, sir.'

'Well, why couldn't I get you ten minutes ago?'

'I was in the middle of a ticklish interview, sir. You see there was this woman, who—'

Angel knew he shouldn't have asked. He would have been given the most unlikely and torturous explanation as to why Crisp had done his good deed for the day.

'I don't want to know,' Angel said. '*I do not want to know*. Put that woman down, and leave anything else you are doing and bring yourself to 33 Melvinia Crescent ASAP.'

'Right, sir.'

Angel cancelled the call, closed the mobile and shoved it back in his pocket. He was still breathing heavily and waiting for the rock in his chest to leave him when Flora and Mrs Fairclough came into the sitting room.

NINE

Susan Fairclough looked round her sitting room uncertainly as if she was seeing it for the first time.

Angel looked up and said, 'It was good of you to come, Mrs Fairclough.'

She looked up at him and forced a smile. She clung on to Flora, who steered her towards an easy chair. She looked at it strangely, then sat down. Flora sat next to her. Angel sat on the settee opposite them.

Don Taylor put his head through the door of the sitting room and said, 'Excuse me, we're off, sir.'

'Right, Don,' Angel said.

He went out and they heard the front door close.

Angel looked across at the trim figure of Susan Fairclough and said, 'There are a few more questions it is necessary for me to ask, if you are up to it?'

She breathed in deeply, straightened her back and stuck out her chest. 'Of course, I am up to it, Inspector.'

He nodded. 'Good. Flora will take notes.'

He looked at her as she nodded and reached down for her bag.

Angel looked at Susan Fairclough. 'Firstly,' he said, 'can you tell me what you did this morning?'

'Yes, certainly,' she said. 'I got up at half past seven, had a shower, got dressed, came downstairs, had breakfast then left here for school at twenty to nine exactly.'

'Did you leave by the front door?'

'Yes. And I locked it. And the back door was already locked, having been locked all night.'

'Thank you, Susan. Please continue.'

'I had classes from nine until half past twelve, when I came home for my lunch.'

'And was the front door locked?'

'No. I wasn't expecting Ian back until late Friday evening, so I had a bit of a shock. The first thing I saw in the hall was that green vacuum cleaner. Then I saw Ian's raincoat on the newel post. I was so pleased. So I called out. Of course, there was no reply. From the hall I saw the fridge door in the kitchen was wide open, so I went in there and—'

She stopped. Her bottom lip quivered.

'You closed it?' Angel said.

She nodded, fished round in her cardigan pocket and pulled out a tissue. She dabbed her eyes.

Angel looked across at Flora. They waited.

'Sorry about that,' Susan Fairclough said.

'That's all right. You found your husband on the floor,' Angel said. 'Did you do anything else before you dialled 999?'

'I cradled his head in my lap and felt for a pulse. I couldn't find one, but I still held him and phoned for the police on my mobile. After a while — they seemed like ages coming — I realized that he had gone and that I couldn't *do* anything, so I got up and wandered round the house, I think. Anyway, I went outside and was on the step when a police car came. Two officers. I couldn't speak. I just pointed the way to the kitchen. One of them asked if I had any family or friendly neighbour nearby. The only one I could think of was Bella — that's Mrs Beasley — at number 28. So, somehow, I arrived there. She's been a darling.'

'There was no sign of a break-in, Susan. Have you any thoughts on how Ian was murdered?'

She frowned, then said, 'Oh. I have just thought of something. When I was wandering round the house, I tidied up this room. Come to think of it, it looked as if there had been a scuffle of some sort. Although Ian was not one to be involved in a fight. That dining chair was tipped over. That lamp had been knocked off the library table and was on the carpet; it wasn't broken, though. Everything on the table was on the floor. This chair and the settee were pushed out of their usual places and some of the cushions on the settee were on the floor. I put everything back in its place.'

Angel rubbed his chin.

'So your husband arrived here this morning sometime after 8.40, with or without the vacuum cleaner. He had a key to let himself in?'

'Yes, of course.'

'His murderer was either waiting for him or . . . he could have knocked on the door. Your husband could have answered it. Say the man was invited in or forced his way in. But having gained access, what did he want?'

'I don't know.'

'You say that your husband is highly unlikely to have bought a vacuum cleaner, and that anyway, you don't need one. The one you have works perfectly well. Well, why would a murderer bring a vacuum cleaner to a house and simply leave it there? Did he expect to make a mess and this was to clean it up afterwards, or what?'

Susan Fairclough looked at him and licked her bottom lip.

Angel ran his hand through his hair and said, 'So now, your husband left Bromersley for London yesterday morning?'

'Well, lunchtime, Inspector. His train left about noon.'

'And you found him this morning at what time?'

'About twenty to one.'

'That's almost twenty-four hours. We need to know where he had been all that time.'

'I have no idea,' Susan Fairclough said.

'Well, can you let me have the telephone number of the London office of where he works and the name of the man he was going to see there? Also do you have a recent head-and-shoulders photograph of Ian you could let us borrow to copy?'

'Certainly. Remind me and I will see that you have both before you leave.'

Angel nodded, and said, 'And will you have a look in the fridge and see if you can see what was taken or what was put in there?'

'Of course,' she said.

She stood up and went into the hall. She hesitated at the entrance to the kitchen, but took a deep breath, stepped forward boldly, not looking down but making straight for the fridge door handle. She pulled it wide open.

She was looking for some time before she said, 'Well, there's nothing been put in, Inspector. Of that, I am sure. I now see that a small pork pie is missing, which is very strange. Also a bottle of semi-skimmed milk.'

'Could your husband have taken them?'

'It doesn't seem likely, Inspector. He's not keen on pastry, particularly pork pie. That was for my lunch today.'

'And the milk?'

'He would have preferred tea.'

Angel rubbed his hand hard across his face. Then he looked down at his notes. 'We have not determined *why* the murderer came to your house. It isn't clear whether he came with the express purpose of murdering Ian, or whether he came for some other purpose . . .'

'What other purpose?' Susan Fairclough said.

'I was hoping you could tell me. Was it to get something from him? It wasn't to rob him. Your Georgian silver tea set on the sideboard is still there. Your antique emerald and diamond ring is still in your dressing-table drawer. Are any of your valuables missing? In fact, is anything missing? Would you have a look round and see?'

'What, now?'

'If you don't mind . . .' Angel said.

Susan Fairclough stood up. She seemed much more confident. She now reassumed the authority of being the householder. She boldly opened and shut a couple of drawers. Then went upstairs.

Angel turned to Flora and said, 'Have you got all that down?'

'Yes, sir,' she said.

Angel's eyes creased. 'I have been thinking,' he said. 'The murderer shot Ian Fairclough between 9.30 and 11.30 this morning. Now, this is a small semi-detached house. The people in the adjoining semi must have heard the shot. You went there this morning, didn't you?'

Flora Carter turned back in her notebook. 'Yes, sir. I did. That was number 31.' She found the page. 'NR,' she said. 'There was no reply. Do you want me to try them again, now?'

'Yes and the other side, number 35.'

She referred to the notebook again. 'I did 35, sir, and they *saw* nothing.'

His face muscles tightened. He clenched his fists. 'Oh hell, Flora. Did they *hear* the gunshot?'

Her face coloured up. She glared back at him. 'It's November *5, Guy Fawkes Day*!' she said. 'There have been bangs all day. And there'll probably be bangs at all hours until after the weekend.'

Angel rubbed his forehead and temple and closed his eyes.

Flora stood up. 'Shall I go and make those calls now?'

Angel was feeling guilty at flying off the handle. Flora was, of course, quite right about the number of explosions there were at this time of the year. He should have thought of it. The only reason why he didn't must have been that he was tired. He looked at his watch. It was 5.15. He had had enough.

'No. Let's pack it in. We've done a lot today.'

'I don't mind, sir, if you want me to?'

He shook his head. 'No. No. We don't think clearly when we're tired, Flora. Do it in the morning. We'll pack up now. You can call on those that were out when I called. I'll give you the list.'

'Right, sir,' she said, looking at her watch. 'Oh, that's great. I didn't want to be late. I'm going to a fireworks party tonight.'

Angel smiled. 'Right. Sounds good. I hope you enjoy yourself.'

Susan Fairclough came in from the hall. She was carrying some clothes, a sponge bag, hairbrush and some other bits. 'Nothing's been taken, Inspector. I've had a good look round.'

Angel nodded.

'I've brought you the last decent photograph of Ian and I've written the name and phone number of his boss at the London office on this bit of paper.'

Angel took them from her, glanced at them and put them in his pocket. 'Thank you,' he said. 'Flora and I are leaving now.'

There was suddenly a burst of pretty-coloured fireworks visible high in the sky through the window, followed by several loud bangs from bangers.

Susan Fairclough flinched at the racket.

Angel said, 'Ah yes. It's Bonfire Night.'

Angel realized belatedly his thoughtlessness, that that racket would be more than usually disturbing for a grieving woman living on her own.

'Oh,' Susan Fairclough said. 'Would you mind seeing me across to Bella's, Inspector? She's kindly giving me a bed for the night.'

'Of course,' he said.

All three made for the door.

It was almost 6 p.m. on Guy Fawkes Night when Angel escorted Susan Fairclough to Bella's house across the road. He then returned to his car. On the way home, he saw a few bonfires with the silhouettes of children dancing round them, some rockets and pretty, golden-rain-type fireworks in the sky and he heard a lot of bangers, some shaking the ground like landmines.

He arrived home at 6.05 p.m.

'You're late, darling,' Mary said, rushing up to him and giving him a kiss on the cheek.

'It's like World War III out there.'

She nodded. 'You've just time to have a beer.'

'If I have a beer, I shall fall asleep. Any post?'

She tilted her head back and looked upwards. 'I've told you,' she said, 'if there was any post it would be on the sideboard.'

He frowned. 'Wouldn't it be easier simply to say "yes"?'

She opened the oven door. 'Erm . . . I don't know,' she said, her mind now on the casserole. She looked around for the oven cloth. She put the hot dish on top of the oven, took off the lid and stirred the contents. She went over to the cupboard.

'Well, obviously it would,' he said. 'A three-letter word is much shorter than, "if there is any post it would be on the sideboard," because, in any case, it usually isn't.'

'Yes, all right, dear,' she said, sprinkling in the gravy thickener. 'Would you like to set the table?'

'Did you hear what I said, Mary?' he said.

'Yes. Will you set the table? It's almost ready,' she said, stirring the thickener in. 'I've had such a day. Went to the hairdresser's this morning, then went down to the station and booked my ticket. I've changed the bed, done the washing and baked an apple pie, a custard and a fruit cake this afternoon. I don't want you starving while I'm away. Miriam goes into the clinic early Friday morning, so I will have to leave early tomorrow morning.'

He looked at her. He still wondered at how beautiful she looked even when her hair was hidden in a turban arrangement and she had a sheen of perspiration on her chin, cheeks and forehead.

'How long are you expecting this lark is going on for?' he said.

'She said two or three days at the most. And it's not a lark.'

'That means you'll be back on Sunday night.'

She pursed her lips and shook her head. 'More like Tuesday. You're forgetting it takes a day to get there, and a day to get back.'

Angel's face went slack and his mouth dropped open. '*Five* days?' he said.

She smiled inwardly. She was flattered that he didn't want to be left. 'You can manage five days without me, can't you?'

'It's for such a *silly* reason. Having her bits and pieces pumped up at her age. Damned ridiculous,' he said, slamming the cutlery drawer. He set out the knives and forks. 'Actually, I have always thought she was adequately endowed in that department.'

Mary smirked. 'Oh, so you've been looking, have you? At *my* sister!'

He shrugged. 'There's no charge for looking, is there? It's not an offence. She's only having it done so that men will look even more. You're a right sexy family if the truth were known.'

But Mary wasn't particularly happy about the operation. 'I hope she'll be all right,' she said. 'The potatoes are done. It's ready. Sit down.'

'She'll be fine,' he said.

'Have you washed your hands?'

He blinked and looked up at her. He lifted his hands, turned his palms uppermost, looked at them, stood up and made for the sink. He ran the hot tap and reached out for the washing-up liquid.

Mary looked back from the oven. 'I don't know why you don't do that in the bathroom. The kitchen sink is *my* domain. And I'm serving up. You're in my way.'

'Won't be a minute.'

He put a splash of the liquid on his palm, rubbed his hands together, swilled them under the tap, turned it off and reached out for the tea towel.

She glared at him. 'Don't use *that* towel!' she said.

He gritted his teeth and continued drying his hands.

She yanked a hand towel down from the clothes rack with such force it caused it to swing and clank on the ceiling. She tossed the towel at him. He didn't try to catch it. It fell on the floor.

'Steady on,' he said. He bent down, picked it up and put it on the back of his chair.

'It doesn't belong *there*,' she said.

His jaw muscles tightened. He sat down at the table.

She snatched it up and threw it back on the rack. It landed askew but safely.

She served up the meal in silence. And there was no conversation until Angel put his knife and fork neatly together on the plate.

'That was very nice, love, thank you,' he said.

She glanced at him and said, 'I'm glad you enjoyed it. Are you still on with that Joan Minter murder?'

'Yep. *And* an armed robbery of a security van. *And* the murder of an insurance man on Melvinia Crescent.'

'Well, you'll hardly notice I've gone then, will you?' she said.

Her hand was on the table. He put his hand on top of hers and said, 'I shall be thinking of you every minute you are away.'

She smiled. 'Oooh,' she said warmly. She leaned over and gave him a kiss on the lips.

There was a moment of quiet. They looked at each other.

He said, 'What time does your train leave?'

'Can you get me to Bromersley Station for 8.10? My connection at Doncaster leaves there at 8.59.'

'Yes. Of course,' he said.

She nodded and smiled. 'You must look after yourself. And keep off the fish and chips. There's a fridge *full* of good, *healthy* food.'

'I'll be all right. Are you all right for money?'

'I withdrew some cash from the hole in the wall on Monday. I've plenty, and I've always my credit card.'

'Ah, Monday,' he said, remembering something. 'You recall that letter that came on Monday? I've been meaning to talk to you about it.'

She frowned. 'No,' she said. 'What was that?'

He reached into his inside pocket and took out the envelope. 'It's from the gas people.'

She pulled a face. 'You're always going on about the gas people,' she said.

His face straightened. 'Of course I am. Their bills are so high now that they virtually have an investment in our lives. Don't you realize that our monthly gas bill is higher than our repayments to the building society?'

Mary glanced up at the ceiling. 'I've heard all this before,' she said.

'No, you haven't, because this has never happened before,' he said. 'The latest thing is this. They say our boiler is more than ten years old and—'

'What exactly is the boiler?'

'That thing on the wall.'

She looked round at it and frowned.

'And they do not guarantee to have spares for it because of its age. Also, if it breaks down, we could be without heating and so on for a week or however long it takes, while they replace it with a new, more efficient boiler, which with all the gubbins would cost us over five thousand pounds.'

Her jaw dropped. Her face paled. 'We can't afford five thousand pounds.'

'I know, but that is the *worst* scenario. What they are saying is that *new* boilers are so efficient that they can save up to twenty per cent of the gas consumed. Also that if we elect to have a new one fitted this month, it could cost up to forty per cent less.'

'That's a consideration,' she said.

He wrinkled his nose. 'It would be, if it were true. We have to consider what we want to do. Every month the gas bills go up.'

'Well I'm sure I can leave it in your capable hands, darling, to do what is best.'

'You can't get away with a bit of old flannel like that,' he said. 'I want to know what you *think*.'

She breathed deliberately in and out before she said, 'You want to know what *I* think? I think you spend far too much time nattering about the gas people and the cost of gas.'

'That's no answer at all. Making decisions requires spending time considering the problem, getting information and weighing up the alternatives before arriving at an answer.'

'There you are,' she said. 'You've just said it. That's what you should do. Get more information.'

Angel's mouth fell open.

She stood up and said, 'Now I have a hundred things to do before I leave in the morning. Must go and wash the pots. Make the coffee, darling, will you?'

Angel rubbed his forehead. He closed his eyes very tightly. His face muscles and veins strained against the skin.

TEN

It was 8.25 when Angel arrived at his office, having driven Mary to Bromersley Station and seen her onto the train. She had given him a myriad of instructions about where things were, what to eat, what not to eat, what to see to, what to leave alone, where to go, where not to go, and what to do in many different and improbable circumstances. He had nodded his understanding of what she had said, fully determined to do exactly as he liked. In fact, much as he loved her and would undoubtedly miss her, he was beginning to think he might enjoy a few days of liberty.

He put his coat on the coat hanger and his hat on the peg and settled down at his desk. He pulled the pile of post and reports forward, determined to begin to reduce it, when the phone rang. It was Mac.

'Michael, I know this is a bit early for you, but—'

Angel said, 'I've been up since six o'clock. What can I do for you?'

'I think it's what I can do for you, Michael,' Mac said. 'When I got yon body of Ian Fairclough on my table, I noticed immediately that the fingers of his right hand were clenched tight, which in itself is not unusual. However, when I peeled back the fingers, there was a button, a black button with a number of cotton threads hanging off it. He must have clenched it tightly and torn it off his assailant.'

Angel's eyes narrowed. In the past, men had been hanged with much less evidence. 'Anything unusual about the button?' he said.

'No, I shouldn't think so. It is a common design in plastic, presumably from a man's raincoat or overcoat. Could have been made just about anywhere in the world. But the thread might be useful. I've run a few tests and I can say that it is cotton, has originated in Egypt, been soaked in sodium hydroxide to shrink it, to increase its lustre and affinity for dye. It would be probable that many cotton threads would be treated like that, but I reckon we could identify a matching thread.'

Angel ran his fingertips across his temple. 'Thank you, Mac. That's great . . . could be a vital clue. You've no further use for the button, I take it?'

'Noo, but I'd need to retain the thread, if I might be required to make a comparison at a later date.'

'Of course, Mac. That would be fine.'

'There are the contents of Ian Fairclough's pockets. You can have those too as soon as you like.'

'Thank you. I'll send somebody across for them and the button this morning. While I have you there, Mac, you remember that the fridge door was found wide open at the Faircloughs' home? Well, it turns out that a pork pie and a pint of milk had been taken. Can you tell me if Ian Fairclough had consumed them in the last three hours of his life?'

Mac hesitated, then said, 'Well, there was certainly no undigested food in his stomach, Michael, but I couldn't be so absolute about the milk. I suppose the alternative explanation is that the murderer took them and was in such a hurry that he didn't close the fridge door.'

'That's what we are thinking, Mac. Thank you.'

'I'll have that stuff ready for collection as soon as you like, Michael. Goodbye.'

Angel replaced the phone. He felt a bit happier. He was thinking that the few small clues he had, put together, could prove a case — if only he had a suspect.

The phone rang again. It was Don Taylor. 'Got an email from the lab, sir,' he said. 'On that cigarette that Joan Minter was smoking when she was shot.'

Angel's eyes brightened. 'Ah yes,' he said.

'It was negative, sir. There was nothing at all unusual about it.'

'Oh,' he said. He sighed and slowly shook his head.

Then Taylor said, 'And that cigarette end recovered from the back of the Slater Security van, Adelaide brand.'

He looked up. 'Yes?'

'They say the sample submitted did not contain a nucleus and therefore DNA was not recoverable.'

'Oh,' he said. 'And what about the champagne glass Joan Minter was holding when she was shot?'

'Negative, sir. It didn't have any additives in it.'

'Right, Don,' Angel said. 'Thank you. Have you heard anything more from Ballistics about the shell case and the Walther from the Joan Minter murder?'

'Ballistics always take a bit longer, sir.'

'Yes, but will you jolly them along?'

'I'll ring up this morning, sir.'

He replaced the phone. Almost everything was negative. His face went slack. He dropped his head. After a few moments, he sighed deeply and dragged the pile of letters, reports and stuff across the desk nearer to him.

There was a knock at the door.

'Come in,' he said.

It was Ahmed. He was carrying a copy of the *Daily Yorkshireman*. 'Good morning, sir. Do you want to see my paper? There's a report on the Ian Fairclough murder across the front page.'

Angel looked up. He did, of course. He was desperately interested. He wanted to see if there were any other traps the informer to the paper had fallen into.

'Can you leave it with me for an hour or so? I have such a lot to see to. Incidentally, there's something I want you to do for me, urgently.'

'Of course, sir,' he said, handing the paper to him.

Angel put it down on his desk. 'Thank you,' he said. Then he took out of his wallet a photograph of Ian Fairclough and the small piece of paper Susan Fairclough had given to him. He looked at the photograph again and passed it up to Ahmed and said, 'Get me six copies as soon as possible.'

'Only take a few minutes, sir,' he said, and he rushed out.

As soon as the door was closed, Angel picked up the copy of the newspaper and looked at the front page. The headline 'Murder in Melvinia!' was splashed across it, with a photograph of the house. He carefully read the text and stopped when he read the words '. . . found in the house, taken there by the killer was a new, green vacuum cleaner'. Who had told the newspaper about that and who had specified that it was green? There was definitely a leak from somebody in the station. He read on. The rest of the text was wordy and sensational.

Angel ran his hand jerkily through his hair. He closed the paper and banged it down at the corner of his desk. That was another irritating little matter he would have to resolve.

He rubbed his chin. He mustn't let that annoying business divert him from the task in hand.

He consulted his notes, then reached out for the phone. He tapped out two single digits and put the phone to his ear.

'Control Room, DS Clifton,' a voice said.

'Bernie,' Angel said. 'Have you any transport going anywhere near the hospital?'

'No trouble to organize that, sir, if you're not in a hurry,' Clifton said.

'Sometime this morning would be fine, Bernie. I want some small items picking up from Dr Mac in the mortuary there, and delivering to me.'

'Leave it with me, sir.'

Angel replaced the phone. He then looked at the small piece of paper Susan Fairclough had given to him. It had a London telephone number and the name John Hooper. He picked up the phone, tapped in a nine for an outside line, then followed it with the number.

A pleasant young woman's voice said, 'Indemnity and Life. Can I help you?'

'Mr John Hooper, please.'

'Thank you. I am connecting you.'

A man's voice came on. 'John Hooper, can I help you?'

Angel introduced himself and told the man the tragic event that had happened the previous day. It came as a shock to Hooper but when he recovered he became an excellent witness.

'Ian was expected here first thing on Wednesday morning,' Hooper said. 'When he didn't arrive I thought he must be ill, but when I hadn't heard anything by yesterday, I phoned his home but I could not get a reply.'

'His wife was sleeping at a neighbour's,' Angel said. 'And I believe that she has now returned to work. I wondered if you could throw any light on the situation. As far as you know, was Ian Fairclough involved with people who walk about armed with guns?'

'Certainly not,' Hooper said. 'Not that I am aware of, anyway. He walked, talked and behaved like the respectable gentleman I am sure he was. This is a long-established family insurance company, Inspector. We deal in domestic house and contents, motor vehicles, holiday and life cover. He has to deal with ordinary members of the public, family men and women, and their children and sometimes grandchildren. They have to trust him to provide the right policy that they need and can afford. We wouldn't have employed him if he had been the slightest bit iffy.'

'Have you any ideas of anyone who would want Ian out of the way?'

'No, Inspector. Certainly not. He was a very hard worker. We were very pleased with him. I cannot imagine him involved with anybody with a gun. It would be so out of character. We are sorry to lose him, particularly in the tragic way you have described.'

'He was away Tuesday night, the fourth. Have you any idea where he might have spent that night?'

'None at all. I left him to make his own arrangements.'

Angel rubbed his chin. 'Did he come up to town often?' he said.

'About four or five times a year, depending on the need.'

'Well, did he not have a regular place where he stayed?'

'I expect he did, Inspector. Yes, of course. I will have to check when he last came, then check on his expenses claim. It will just take me a couple of minutes.'

'I'll hold,' Angel said.

Several minutes later, Angel had an address and a phone number for a small two-star hotel in WC1.

He thanked Hooper, ended the call and tapped in the phone number of the hotel.

'The De Coverley Hotel,' the lady said.

Angel introduced himself and asked her if Ian Fairclough had stayed at the hotel the previous Tuesday night.

'I will have to look. One moment, please . . . Yes, he did,' she said.

Angel said, 'And can you tell me if he was on his own?'

She hesitated, then said, 'Well, yes. He was in room number 114, which is a single room. It also looks as if he was originally booked in for last night as well, that would have been two nights, but he must have cancelled.'

'Have you any idea *why* he cancelled?'

'Sorry, sir. No idea. We are rather busy here.'

'That must have put you out quite a bit?'

'Not at all. If somebody wants to cancel, we don't question why. Provided they clear the room by 10 a.m. and pay their bill. We normally have no difficulty reletting it.'

'Was there anything unusual about his behaviour?'

'Nobody said anything, sir. We don't pry. But I really don't know. Sorry.'

Angel ended the call. He rubbed his chin with his fingertips and nodded. He was satisfied that Ian Fairclough had spent the Tuesday night he was missing at the De Coverley Hotel in London. That was clear enough. Angel leaned back in his chair. His face creased and he wrinkled his nose. He was thinking that it didn't explain why Fairclough came back a day early, why he came to be found murdered in his own home the next day, nor why there was a new, unwanted vacuum cleaner found in the house.

The phone rang. He reached out for it. 'Angel,' he said.

It was Flora Carter. She sounded as if she had been running. 'I'm on Melvinia Crescent, sir, catching up on the on the door to door. I've come across a witness who said that at about ten o'clock yesterday morning she was in her front bedroom when she saw a salesman walking up the path of number 33. He was a big man with broad shoulders, in a black or dark-grey overcoat. She saw him knock at the front door.'

Angel's eyebrows shot up. A tiny volcano erupted in the middle of his chest, spreading hot lava throughout his upper body. 'What else did she see?'

'That's all, sir.'

'What was the colour of his hair?'

'She didn't notice.'

'Was he in a car or a van?'

'She doesn't know, sir,' Flora said. 'I've got as much out of her as I can.'

Angel wrinkled his nose. 'Right, Flora. Thank you. That's great. Finish off the rest of the houses. Somebody else might have seen him. Then come back here.'

'Right, sir,' she said.

Angel ended the call and returned the phone to its cradle. He rubbed his hands. It was a breakthrough, at last. The news restored his faith that he could solve at least one of the murder cases.

It was more than an hour later when Angel's phone rang out.

He snatched it up. 'Angel,' he said.

It was the civilian receptionist, Mrs Meredew. 'Sorry to bother you, Inspector, but I've had lots of enquiries from the press and television news companies for information about the Joan Minter and the Ian Fairclough murders. They usually ask for you. I've always told them what you instructed me to say, that you are out and that I never know when you are coming back in. However, some of them are getting impatient and suspect that you are avoiding them. I know you like to keep the right side of them, so I wondered if you wanted to speak to any of them, or if you wanted to change the instruction?'

Angel creased his eyes and went through the motions of whistling silently. Then he said, 'You're quite right. I don't want to antagonize any of them, but I really haven't the time. I suppose you can say that when I have made any progress in either case, I'll be making a statement or calling a press conference. That should keep them happy.'

'That sounds better, Inspector,' she said. 'All right, that's what I'll say from now on. Thank you.'

She rang off. As soon as he cancelled the call, the phone rang out again. It was Susan Fairclough.

'I thought I should ring you and let you know that I've been back to my house,' she said. 'I steeled myself this morning and went back in there. I wanted to get myself and my home back into something like order. I can't spend the rest of my life being a moping widow.'

'That's good,' Angel said, 'but there's no real hurry, Susan. You must take your changed life a day at a time, as they say.'

'Yes . . . well, I'm glad that I did. Because I've realized that the overnight case that Ian took with him to London is missing. It's not in the house anywhere.'

Angel pursed his lips. His eyebrows went up. 'Hmm. Was there anything valuable in it?'

'No. Just what you'd expect for two nights away on business. Nightclothes and washing and shaving tackle, toothbrush, clean shirts, that sort of thing.'

Angel ran his fingers across his forehead. 'Was Ian a forgetful sort of person? Did he leave things behind on the train or in the hotel or . . . ?'

'No, Inspector, not at all. He was likely to consider them far too costly to treat casually like that.'

Angel nodded. 'Hmmm. I can't think of the significance of that, if there is anything, but thank you, Susan, for letting me know.'

They ended the call.

Angel replaced the phone and scratched his head. Successful insurance was a bit like successful detection work. It was all about detail, and Angel was thinking that the Indemnity and Life Insurance Company would not have been so delighted with Ian Fairclough if he had not paid proper attention to the nitty-gritty details of his customers' needs and the myriad conditions and exceptions of insurance companies' policies. Likewise, he was positive that the man would not have been casual about the whereabouts of his overnight bag of clean clothes and washing tackle.

He was still thinking about this when there was a knock at the door. It was Ahmed. He was carrying a polythene bag with the word 'Evidence' printed boldly across it, another small bag and some sheets of A4 paper.

'I've got those six copies of the photograph of Ian Fairclough you wanted, sir,' he said. 'And a patrolman handed in this evidence bag and this little bag from the mortuary.'

'Thank you, Ahmed,' Angel said.

The young man went out.

Angel looked at the button in the small bag first. It was totally unexceptional. He stood up and crossed to his own overcoat that was on the peg secured onto the side of the green stationery cupboard. He compared the button to those on his own coat. It was near enough the same colour and appearance, but looking at it closely, there were several small differences in the shape, size and patination. He wrinkled his nose, dropped the button into his pocket and returned to the desk. He opened the evidence bag and tipped the contents out. There was a key that looked like a house key, several coins, a mobile phone, a car key, a handkerchief, and a leather wallet containing cash, driving licence, two credit cards and several business cards. He looked at the contents carefully, then checked over everything again. It all looked perfectly ordinary. There was nothing there to suggest anything different.

He leaned back in the chair and rubbed his chin. His mind wandered away from the contents of Ian Fairclough's pockets. There were so many loose ends. He wanted to go to Bromersley railway station with the photograph of Fairclough. But something was niggling him. It was something that Flora had said about an hour ago. He remembered the words. They were: 'A witness had said that at about ten o'clock yesterday morning, she saw a salesman walking up the path of number 33. He was a big man with broad shoulders, in a black or dark-grey overcoat.' That wasn't right. It needed some explanation.

He took out his mobile and phoned her.

'You wanted me, sir?' Flora said.

'About what you said earlier,' he said. 'How did the witness know that the big man with the broad shoulders was a salesman?'

Flora hesitated. 'I suppose she assumed he was, sir,' she said.

Angel squeezed the lobe of his ear and pulled it a few times and said, 'What's the name of the witness, Flora?'

'Mrs Emily Watson. She lives at number 30, next door to Bella Beasley.'

ELEVEN

Angel rang the doorbell and a wide-eyed woman opened the door.

He smiled at her and said, 'Mrs Watson, Mrs Emily Watson? I'm DI Angel, Bromersley Police. I believe my sergeant came earlier this morning.'

'Yes,' she said. 'Is everything all right?'

'Oh yes. It's good that we have such wide-awake and observant citizens like you around to assist us in our work.'

'Come in, Mr Angel,' she said, standing back and pulling the door handle.

'Thank you,' he said. 'There's just one little thing about your statement. You told my sergeant that the man you saw was a salesman. I just wondered why you said that.'

'Well, I believe he was. He was dressed the part and he was carrying something. I couldn't see exactly what it was. It could have been a garden hosepipe with a spade or a fork. From the angle I was seeing him, his body was shielding it as he walked up the path. He carried it in his right hand, you see. Does it matter? I'm sure he *was* a salesman.'

Angel felt his pulse quicken. He felt a lightness in the chest. 'Will you show me the window you saw this through?'

'Certainly. It's up the stairs. Will you follow me?'

He was shown into the front bedroom and saw that Mrs Watson would have had an excellent view of a man walking up the path. But her view of what he was carrying, if it had been in his right hand and held close, would be mostly out of sight.

'What makes you think it might have been a garden hose?' he said.

'Well, the colour. It was a bright green.'

Angel grinned. 'Bright green?' he said.

'Well, green anyway. There are a lot of greens.'

Angel scratched his head. 'Indeed there are,' he said. Then he added, 'Are you going out at all, Mrs Watson?'

'No. I shall be in all day, why?'

'I want to show you something. I'll be back in ten minutes or so,' he said. 'Will that be convenient to you?'

Ten minutes later he rang Mrs Watson's doorbell again. He smiled at her and said, 'I have organized a re-enactment of what I believe you saw yesterday. Can we go back upstairs?'

Mrs Watson's forehead creased. 'Well yes, erm, I suppose.'

'It won't take above a couple of minutes,' he said.

When they were in position, Angel opened his phone, scrolled down to a number, clicked on it and said, 'Right, John. Carry on.' Then he closed the phone.

He turned to Mrs Watson and said, 'Keep your eye on the path to number 33.'

Immediately they saw a big man in a raincoat arrive at the gate of the Faircloughs' house. He was carrying the green vacuum cleaner in his right hand and keeping it close to his side. He opened the gate, walked up the path to the front door, rang the bell, waited, then walked into the house.

Angel looked at Mrs Watson.

She was frowning. She didn't look happy.

He ran his hand through his hair. 'Isn't that what you saw yesterday?' he said.

'No. The man I saw was wearing a *black* coat. And he was *bigger* than that man.'

'I understand that,' Angel said. 'That raincoat was the only coat we could get to fit at short notice, but is *that* what you saw being carried up the path?'

'Oh yes. And that's exactly the right shade of green.'

Angel smiled. He felt a slight flutter of excitement in his chest. He now had an eye-witness account of a man (and a basic description of him) entering the victim's house at the time of his murder.

He thanked her, left the house, got into his car and went straight down to Bromersley railway station. He went up to the ticket-office window, showed his badge and ID and said, 'Can I see the station manager, please?'

The clerk turned to a man behind him. 'There's a policeman to see you, Stan.'

The door at the side of the window opened and another man came out. He wore a hat that had the word 'Stationmaster' in gold on it. He looked at Angel, took the hat off, scratched his head, put it back on again and said, 'What's the matter, Constable?'

Angel produced a picture of Ian Fairclough and showed it to him. 'Do you recognize this man? I believe he travelled by train from here to London on Tuesday morning and then returned probably yesterday morning.'

'Come on in,' the stationmaster said.

Angel stepped into the office and closed the door.

The stationmaster looked at the photograph and said, 'No. I don't remember him. We see hundreds of faces every day. Can't remember them all, you know.'

Angel wrinkled his nose.

'Just a minute,' the stationmaster said.

He took the photograph to the man on the stool at the little window. 'Hey, Jim. He's asking if we've seen this joker anywhere lately.'

'He'll be that guy with the fancy suitcase that big detective was looking for. He looks as pure as the driven snow, but underneath I bet he's a real monster.'

Angel pursed his lips. He tilted his head to one side. 'What's all this?'

'Yesterday, it was,' the man on the stool said. 'One of your lot came with a photograph of a crowd of people. Looked like it was taken on a station platform somewhere. Probably blown up from a CCTV picture. There was this man in the distance carrying this brown and white suitcase. I didn't remember him, but I remembered the suitcase.'

'What did this man who said he was a detective look like?'

'You'll know him. He's one of *your* lot. He was big. Broad in the shoulders. He wore a black overcoat. Looked as if he'd been hit in the face with a shovel. He said that he was looking for the man with the brown and white suitcase. Looks like it's the same man you are looking for.'

Angel's heart began to race. 'And were you able to help him?' he said.

'Yeah. I had seen the man — well, I mean I'd seen the suitcase — arrive on the 10.13 from Doncaster. I took his ticket. I seem to remember it was from King's Cross.'

'You told him that?'

'Yeah. Then I saw him make for the taxi rank. So *he* pushed off straight to the taxi rank.'

'What did he do then?'

'I don't know. I was busy checking off all the tickets . . . make sure I hadn't missed anybody.'

'Right. Thank you. You've been very helpful.'

The man on the stool grinned and said, 'Well, tell your patrolman not to give me a ticket if I happen to be going at thirty-two miles an hour on the ring road in the middle of the night.'

Angel grinned. 'I'm only a constable,' he said. 'I can't do anything about that.' He came out of the ticket office and went straight outside to the taxi rank.

There were three taxis waiting. He went down each car in turn. He showed the driver the photograph of Ian Fairclough, described the suitcase and told them about the big man with very broad shoulders wearing a black overcoat. None of them could remember seeing anything at all that he had mentioned.

He turned away.

The trail stopped there.

His face went slack and his mouth fell open.

He was thinking about what to do next when he noticed that another taxi had arrived and was unloading some passengers.

Angel advanced towards the driver. He took out his badge and ID and showed it to the driver. Then he went into the spiel.

At first the driver shook his head, then he said, 'Yesterday morning? About this time? Yeah. I told him I remembered the suitcase and taking the man in the photograph to Melvinia Crescent. I couldn't remember the number of the house, but I thought I would be able to find it if I went back there. He jumped in the cab and told me to take him there. Anyway, we were going along Wakefield Road and as we were passing Cheapo's, the supermarket, he suddenly said he wanted to call there and get something, so I took him there. He asked me to wait, so I did. He came out with a vacuum cleaner. He said it had been in a sale.'

Angel's jaw muscles stiffened. 'What did this man look like?'

The driver frowned. 'Don't *you* know? He was one of *your* men. He was big. Got a face like a boxer. Big nose. Big ears. Tall and he had broad shoulders. He was wearing a black overcoat.'

Angel's lips tightened back against his teeth. 'He wasn't a policeman,' he said grimly. 'He murdered the man in the photograph.'

The driver froze. He put a hand across his chest as if he had a pain. 'Are you sure?' he said.

'Positive. And it's my job to catch him. Do you think you could find the house you took him to on Melvinia Crescent?'

'Yeah. No problem.'

Several minutes later, the taxi pulled up outside 33 Melvinia Crescent. Angel had followed him in the BMW. He stopped, got out and walked up to the taxi driver's window.

The driver saw Angel approaching. 'This is it,' the driver said. 'I stopped here. He got out with the vacuum cleaner, paid me and I drove away. I never saw him again or thought any more about it until you asked me just now.'

'What do I owe you?' Angel said.

'Forget it. It was a pleasure. Catching the bastard will be worth a million times more than the cost of the journey. I hope you catch him very soon,' the driver said. Then with a wave of the hand he drove away.

Angel watched him go. 'So do I,' he muttered to himself. 'Before he catches me.'

He looked up at the house and wondered if Susan Fairclough was in. He had a few questions for her.

He made his way up the path and rang the bell.

She opened the door on the chain and was delighted to see that Angel was her visitor.

'Oh, it's you, Inspector. Oh do come in. You're just in time for coffee.'

'Thank you,' he said. 'I'd like to return that photograph of Ian you lent me.'

'Go into the sitting room and sit down. I won't be a minute. The kettle has just boiled.'

'That's very nice,' he said. 'There are a few questions I'd like to put to you while I'm here.'

'Of course, Inspector. Anything I can do to help. Make yourself comfortable.'

After a few moments she brought the coffee through. When they were settled she said, 'Now then, you wanted to ask me something?'

'Yes. Can you describe Ian's suitcase for me?'

'Oh, it was very smart. It was brand new. It was white and brown leather, well, simulated leather. Probably plastic. I bought it from a catalogue.'

He nodded.

‘Why? Is it important?’ she said.

Could be,’ Angel said. ‘You wouldn’t happen to have the catalogue, would you?’

‘Might have,’ she said, leaning down to the magazine rack on the floor by the side of the easy chair. She pulled out a few magazines, catalogues and a newspaper, discarded everything except one particular catalogue, whizzed through the pages and eventually came to the page she wanted. She passed the catalogue over to Angel, pointed to the illustration of a two-tone suitcase and said, ‘There. That’s the one.’

Angel looked at it and said, ‘Can I have this illustration?’

‘Tear out the page,’ she said.

He hesitated. She took the catalogue from him, tore out the page, handed it to him and tucked the catalogue back in the magazine rack.

‘Thank you.’

He looked at it again, then put it in his inside pocket between his wallet and an envelope.

‘Is that significant?’ she said.

‘It might be,’ he said, sipping the coffee. ‘Tell me, Susan, was your husband carrying anything valuable in the suitcase . . . so valuable that crooks might be interested in it?’

‘No, Inspector. Not that I know about. We are not rich. We both had jobs. We were nicely fixed in these hard times, but we’ve nothing of any value. Certainly nothing worth murdering for.’

‘He wasn’t carrying anything for a third party?’

‘You mean like a courier?’ Her eyes suddenly narrowed, then opened wide. ‘You mean *drugs*?’ she said.

‘Well, drugs, money, gold, anything?’

‘No. No. Not Ian,’ she said. ‘He was far too honest and . . . and far too staid, if the truth were known.’

Angel thought about her reply a few moments, then he said, ‘Have you any idea at all why your husband set off from here on Tuesday, ostensibly to spend two nights in London, then in fact spent only one night there and returned early on Wednesday morning?’

Susan Fairclough stared at Angel open-mouthed. 'Certainly not, Inspector. Ian was an absolutely genuine man. I'm sure of that,' she said, splaying a hand across her upper chest. 'He wouldn't do anything at all dishonest. You can be certain of that, Inspector. I don't think he ever did a dishonest thing in his life. He was as near perfect as any human could be.'

Angel was reminded of one of the only two quotations he could remember from Shakespeare. It was: 'The lady doth protest too much, methinks.'

He came out of the Faircloughs' house not much wiser than when he went in. He turned the car into Park Road and headed towards Cheapo's. He had that lead to follow up, too. As he drove along, he was encouraged by the information that had been fed back to him from SOCO, and from witnesses, concerning the Ian Fairclough murder, but was dismayed that there had been so little forthcoming about the Joan Minter case. Following his present lines of inquiry the only information outstanding was from Ballistics. He had already had the account of the history of the Walther used in that murder. There was really only confirmation (or otherwise) that the bullet case had actually come from that gun. Whatever Ballistics said, he couldn't see that it would open a fresh line of inquiry.

He was still thinking the whole situation over when he turned off the main road and into the massive car park at the front of Cheapo's. He parked up and went into the store. He showed his ID and badge, asked for the manager and was shown into his office.

'I need your help regarding enquiries I am making into a recent murder case,' Angel said.

The young manager said, 'We'll do anything we can to assist you, Inspector.'

'I have information to say that a man bought a green vacuum cleaner here sometime between 10.15 and 11 a.m. yesterday morning,' Angel said. 'I want to know what he looked like. Can I see your CCTV for yesterday morning?'

'Certainly,' the manager said. 'That should be easy to find. We could look at the tape from the main door, and if he isn't there, he'll most certainly be on the tape from the electrical department.'

He picked up the phone, explained what was required, and a few minutes later a young man came into the office with two tapes in his hand. The manager introduced the two men and then settled back in his chair and watched the proceedings.

The young man dropped one of the tapes into a projector, switched it on, then, pointing to a seat facing the office wall, said, 'Would you like to sit here, Inspector? You will see better.'

Angel settled into position in a chair facing the wall.

'This is the recording of yesterday morning's CCTV of the main door, Inspector,' the young man said.

A picture suddenly appeared on the screen.

The manager closed the office blinds.

The picture simply showed a steady flow of people coming in and going out of the store through the big automatic sliding doors. The time of the recording was shown on the corner of the screen. It said 9.30 a.m.

Angel said, 'Can you run it on to about 10.15, please?'

'Certainly,' the young man said. The picture skidded across the screen. 'What exactly are we looking for, Inspector?'

'A man with a green vacuum cleaner leaving the store.'

The manager said, 'Hmm. Did he pay for it?'

'I don't know,' the young man said.

Angel said, 'So sorry. I have no idea either.'

Then he heard the manager behind him pick up the phone. 'Mrs Rubens, please . . . Ah, Mrs Rubens? I have a police inspector in my office. He is urgently trying to trace a man who left the store with a green vacuum cleaner yesterday morning between 10.15 and 11 a.m. He doesn't know whether he paid for it or not. Let's assume he did. Will you quickly check the till receipts in the electrical department and tell me the exact time on the receipt? . . . Yes, the *time*. And ring me back. Quick as you can, Mrs Rubens, thank you.' He replaced the phone.

The young man slowed the tape; the time showed 10.25 a.m.

'That's fine, thank you,' Angel said, and he stared at the screen. It mostly showed women with children, pushing shopping trolleys laden with purchases. The store became busier and busier and customers were crowding in and out at the same time. Then suddenly in the fray was the back view of a big man in a dark overcoat with a lot of black hair holding high a green vacuum cleaner. In a second he was enveloped into the crowd that flowed through the door and out of the picture.

Angel could hardly control himself. There was a solid drumming in his chest. '*There* he is,' he said. 'That's the man. Can you stop the tape?'

The time on the tape was 10.29 a.m.

The young man looked at him and smiled. He replayed the tape, but Angel had to be content with only the back view of the man holding the vacuum cleaner.

Angel looked at the store manager and said, 'Will you send me a copy of that piece of tape, sir?'

'Indeed I will, Inspector,' the manager said. 'In fact you can take the whole tape with you now.'

'That's very kind. Thank you,' he said.

'If I now run the tape from the electrical department and fast forward up to, say, 10.15 a.m.,' the young man said, 'that would be about the time he was there, wouldn't it?'

Angel nodded. 'I should think so,' he said, rejuvenated by the shot of adrenaline surging round his system.

As the young man began to change the tapes the phone behind them rang. The manager reached out for it.

'Yes, Mrs Rubens,' he said. 'Oh good . . . yes, got that . . . and it *was* paid for, good . . . And how was it paid? . . . Right.' He replaced the phone.

'Inspector,' he said. 'You'll be pleased to know that the vacuum cleaner was paid for in cash at 10.26 yesterday morning.'

'Thank you,' Angel said; however, he would have much preferred the transaction to have been executed by credit card or cheque. The documents would have given him new avenues to investigate.

'10.26,' the young man said. 'Let's start around 10.20.'

'Right,' Angel said.

The tape was soon run on and they carefully watched it up to and including the time the till receipt was printed. There were pictures of other customers in the department but there was no sign of the big man with a vacuum cleaner. The young man ran the tape forward and backward several times covering earlier and later times, but the big man was not on the screen.

Angel gritted his teeth and ran his hand through his hair.

The manager said, 'Have you got the right *day*? It was only yesterday, Wednesday.'

The young man said, 'Yes. He must have been aware of this particular camera and been working round it.'

'That is possible,' the manager said. Then he turned to Angel and said, 'I'm sorry, Inspector. I hope we have been of *some* help.'

Angel stood up. He waved the tape he had been given and said, 'Indeed you have.'

'I hope you catch the man, Inspector.'

'Thank you.'

TWELVE

Angel returned to the station. He was working in his office when there was a knock at the door.

'Come in,' Angel said.

It was Don Taylor. He was holding a letter.

'Yes, Don,' Angel said. 'What's that you've got?'

'It's a report from Ballistics, sir. Just come in by courier from Wetherby.'

'What's it say?'

'Well, sir, it goes around the houses a bit, but essentially it says that the firing pin in the Walther matches the bullet case found in Joan Minter's drawing room . . .'

'In other words it proves that the Walther was used to kill Joan Minter.'

'Yes, sir, but we had already assumed that, hadn't we?'

Angel pulled a tired, unhappy face. 'When are we going to get a break with this case?'

Taylor knew the feeling. It had happened many times. 'It will come, sir. It will come. For you, sir. It always has.' He turned and made for the door.

Angel looked at him and smiled, then said, 'I'll tell you something, Don. You've got more confidence in me than I have.'

Taylor smiled and went out.

Angel sat back in the chair, closed his eyes and massaged his temples with his fingertips. He stayed like that for a few minutes. Then he slowly opened his eyes, got to his feet, put on his coat and hat and left the office.

He passed the cells to the back entrance straight onto the police car park. He got into the BMW and drove it to 24 Ceresford Road. The gate was open so he drove straight onto the long gravel drive, round the cluster of pine trees and bushes of rhododendrons and all the way up to the front of the house. He got out of the car, walked across the gravel and up the stone steps to the door and rang the bell.

The door was a long time being answered. It was eventually opened three inches on a chain by a woman.

'Who are you and what do you want?' the voice said.

'Mrs Sellars?' he said.

'Yes,' she said.

Angel introduced himself and showed her his ID and his badge through the gap. 'I wanted to ask you about the robbery of your handbag,' he said.

She took off the chain and pulled open the door. 'I am so sorry to appear to be so unfriendly, Inspector, but after my experience I am very wary.'

'Quite right too,' he said.

'Please come in.'

She showed him into the sitting room and gestured to him to take a seat. She sat in the easy chair opposite. On the carpet by her chair he saw a black leather handbag. She reached down for it, opened it, took out a lighter and a packet of cigarettes. She opened the packet and offered him a cigarette.

Angel put up a hand and said, 'No, thanks.' Then he noticed the word 'Adelaide' printed in dark blue on the packet.

'Would you like a cup of tea?' she said.

'No, thanks,' he said.

She put a cigarette in her mouth and clicked the lighter.

He stared at her and then at the pack of cigarettes in the top of the open bag. He had been thrown somewhat off his stride. He hadn't heard of the Adelaide brand until a butt had been found by SOCO in the back of the Slater Security van at Hemmsfield.

She inhaled the cigarette, blew out a cloud of smoke, sighed and settled back in the chair.

Angel pursed his lips. 'I wonder if I may look at the cigarette packet,' he said, pointing towards the handbag.

She frowned, then smiled. She leaned forward, picked it out of her bag and passed it to him. 'Am I tempting you, Inspector? Please help yourself.'

'Oh no,' he said. 'I stopped smoking around ten years ago. It was a great struggle. I would never start again.'

He took the packet, pushed open the bottom, took out a cigarette to see that it was branded at the top like the butt found. It was. He replaced the cigarette, closed the packet and checked the printing on it. It said: 'Made from pure blended Virginian tobacco. Packed in Adelaide, Australia, for export.'

He looked at Mrs Sellars and said, 'Do you mind telling me where you bought them?'

'Not at all,' she said. 'They were a present, actually. My son brought them back for me from Australia. He went on a working holiday down there. Came back a week ago. They are very nice . . . quite mild.'

Angel handed her back the packet. 'Thank you,' he said. 'I have never heard of them.'

'Nor had I,' she said. 'My son said that they're only sold in Australia.'

Angel nodded. 'Now, Mrs Sellars, I have read the statement you gave to my sergeant on Monday and he told me you had looked through our rogues' gallery and not found the thief who knocked on your front door.'

'That's right. I'm sure he wasn't there.'

'I wonder if I could ask you — in your own words — to describe him to me.'

'Well, Inspector, he was just a young man, in the inevitable jeans, plain blue T-shirt, fawn-coloured car coat, thin build . . . and that's about it.'

Angel took out the old brown envelope from his inside pocket and made notes on it in very small, neat writing.

'No shoes? No hat?'

'I think he was wearing trainers . . . white trainers . . . well, they had once been white. Yes, he was. No hat. He had dark hair. He had a beard — well, no, not a beard, a few days' growth.'

He shook his head. 'The girls like that unkempt look. In my day, we would have been called scruffy. Anything else?'

'No. I don't think so.'

'How old do you think he was?'

'About thirty, I should think.'

'Thirty, right,' he said, and put it in his notes. 'Any tattoos, jewellery, earrings, medallions . . . ?'

'No, I don't think so,' she said, her eyebrows lowered and her face tightened. Then she added, 'He had an awful ring on his right hand. It was a skull . . . in what looked like silver.'

Angel's face brightened. 'That could help,' he said. 'How big was it?'

'About as big as a ten-pence piece.'

'Thank you very much,' he said.

Angel arrived back at his office at three o'clock. He hung up his coat and hat and sat down at his desk. He picked up the phone and dialled Ahmed. 'Come into my office.'

'Right, sir,' he said, and a minute later he was there.

'Ahmed, I want you to get onto the PNC website and check villains who are known to wear a silver ring — or any jewellery or symbol — in the form of a skull.'

Ahmed blinked. 'A skull, sir,' he said. 'Have you found a suspect, sir?'

'I might have. See what you can find.'

Ahmed nodded and rushed off.

A few moments later there was a knock at the door.

'Come in,' Angel called.

It was DS Flora Carter. 'I've finished the door to door, sir. I've covered every house now. I went back to number

31 just to make sure. There was nobody in the house the morning of the fifth, so they wouldn't have heard anything anyway. And the man in number 35 said that they may have heard a gunshot, but there were bangs celebrating Guy Fawkes all day and most of the evening and night, so they really couldn't be sure.'

'Right,' Angel said. 'I think we are now assured that the only neighbour to see anything was Mrs Watson across the road from the Faircloughs.'

'I think so, sir.'

'Right. Now let's move on. Sit down a minute.'

When she was settled, he said, 'I've been to see Mrs Sellars.'

She looked up at him in surprise. 'Yes, sir?'

'Yes. And I noticed she smoked Adelaide cigarettes. I don't remember you making any mention of the fact.'

Her forehead creased, she shook her head and said, 'Only because I didn't know, sir.'

'Have you the list of—'

There was a knock at the door. 'Come in,' Angel said.

It was DC Scrivens. He was carrying a pickaxe. 'Oh, sorry to interrupt, sir.'

'You're not interrupting, Ted. Come in. Hang on a minute.'

He turned back to Flora and said, 'Have you got that list of the contents of Mrs Sellars' handbag?'

'No, sir. It's on a statement form. On my desk.'

'Fetch it, will you? I need to see it.'

Flora Carter stood up, went out and closed the door.

Angel turned back to Scrivens. 'Now, Ted, what success have you had with those pickaxes?'

'None, sir. I've called on every hardware shop, garden centre, supermarket and shop I could think of. It occurred to me that they may have been bought online.'

Angel breathed in and out noisily. 'Maybe, lad, maybe. Well, we can't contact every outlet on the internet that might sell pickaxes. There will be an appeal in the *Bromersley*

Chronicle on Friday. That might produce a result. Right, well, leave that pickaxe here and get back to what you were doing.'

'Right, sir.'

As Scrivens went out, Flora Carter came in, waving a sheet of paper. 'Got it here, sir,' she said, passing the single A4 page of the witness's statement over to him.

He turned over the page and found the list. He noticed the length of it, looked up at Flora and said, 'All this in *one* handbag? Is it . . . er, usual . . . er, normal?'

Flora smiled. 'Well, there was nothing there that surprised me, sir,' she said.

Angel's eyes scanned the list rapidly, looked up at Flora, then scanned it again. 'There's no mention of cigarettes, or matches or lighter.'

'They are not there, sir, because *she* didn't mention them.'

'But she was puffing away when I saw her, *and* she was smoking those Adelaide-brand cigarettes.'

Flora swallowed several times, then put her hands out palms uppermost. 'I don't have an answer, sir. I can't explain it. She simply didn't mention them. If she had I would have written them down.'

Angel clenched his teeth, shook the witness's statement and said, 'What's her telephone number?'

'It's at the top over the page, sir,' she said, pointing at the statement.

He found it straightaway, reached out, picked up the phone and tapped it in. It was soon answered.

'Inspector Angel here, Mrs Sellars.'

'Back so soon, Inspector. What can I do for you?'

'Well, on Tuesday last you gave my sergeant a list of the contents of your handbag stolen from your kitchen.'

'Yes, Inspector, that's right. Is there anything wrong?'

Angel blew out a length of breath and said, 'It may not be wrong exactly, Mrs Sellars, but you neglected to include your cigarettes and lighter.'

She didn't answer straight away. Eventually she said, 'Erm, well, yes, Inspector. There were two packs of cigarettes, a full pack and a part pack, say around thirty cigarettes, and my old silver Dunhill lighter.'

'And were the cigarettes Adelaide, the same brand you were smoking this afternoon?'

'As a matter of fact, they were,' she said.

He licked his bottom lip with the tip of his tongue. 'Why didn't you include the cigarettes and lighter in the list of contents of your handbag you gave to my sergeant?'

She took a deep breath, then said, 'Well, the truth is, Inspector, my husband does not like me to smoke. So I never smoke in front of him. And I wasn't sure if he might possibly for some reason in the future see that list.'

'Oh,' Angel said. 'So you smoke on the sly?'

'It's crude of you to put it like that, Inspector. But yes, that's how it is.'

'Right. Thank you, Mrs Sellars. Goodbye.'

As he replaced the phone it immediately rang out. Angel picked it up. 'Angel,' he said.

The sound of coughing indicated that it was his immediate superior, Superintendent Horace Harker, on the line. It never was a pleasant experience. Angel's eyes narrowed. His face tightened. He rubbed his brow.

'There you are,' Harker said between bouts of coughing and wheezing. 'I've been trying to get you for half an hour. You're always on the phone. I hope you weren't ringing Hong Kong.'

'It was just a local call, sir,' Angel said.

'Never mind about that,' he grunted. 'Come up here. *Now!*'

Before Angel could reply, the line went dead.

Angel gritted his teeth. He replaced the phone and turned to Flora Carter. He breathed out noisily while slowly shaking his head. 'That was the super,' he said. 'He wants to see me *now*. I'll speak to you later.'

'Right, sir,' she said.

Angel detested interviews with Superintendent Harker. They never proved helpful or pleasant. He went out of his office and tramped up the green-painted corridor to the door at the end which had the words 'Detective Superintendent Horace Harker' painted on it. He knocked on the door.

'Come in,' Harker called.

Angel pushed open the door and immediately found himself in an environment of warm, moving air, reeking of menthol. Although he was not unused to it, his natural reaction was to blink, which he did several times until he became accustomed to it.

He went up to the big desk covered with box files, ledgers, piles of letters, envelopes, pens, pencils, elastic bands, copies of the *Police Gazette*, cotton-wool balls, a bottle of Gaviscon, a jar of Vicks, a telephone, a bottle opener, a telephone directory, box of Kleenex, a box of Movicol, a screwdriver, a pair of woollen tartan socks and so on.

Behind the desk was the superintendent. His head was like a skull with big ears.

'Sit down, lad,' Harker said, picking up a sheet of A4 from the many at his fingertips. 'Now then, you are investigating two suspect murders, aren't you? Tell me in a few words the progress you are making.'

'Yes, sir. But you will know all this from my reports. The first case is the shooting of Joan Minter. I cannot claim a great deal of progress with solving this case. There seem to be quite a few people in the business who have an intense dislike of her, but there aren't any witnesses or corroborative witnesses to anything. Also there isn't any forensic evidence on which to begin to build a case.'

'Haven't you any suspects at all?'

'Well, yes. There's Felix Lubrecki, an actor. There was also a man called Charles Fachinno. He had made a fortune out of potted meat.'

Harker looked as if he'd just come out of an exhumation tent and was about to throw up. 'Potted meat?' he said.

'Yes, sir. In those little moulded glass jars—'

His face tightened. '*I know. I know*,' he said. '*I know* what potted meat is.'

'He's dead now,' Angel said, 'Also Leo Altman, another actor. And a prominent producer, Erick Cartlett.'

Harker said, 'All right, all right. That's enough. What about the other case?'

'The other case is the murder of Ian Fairclough,' Angel said. 'A man found in his own home, also killed by a gunshot. Can't find a motive for his murder. Again, there's no forensic, but the dead man was found to have a black overcoat button in his closed fist. But it's a very common colour and size. However, if we can arrest a suspect, and he has a missing button on his coat, then it would become a powerful piece of evidence. Also, we have a witness and some CCTV of the man we believe is the murderer. Unfortunately the picture is only of his back. However, he is wearing a black overcoat.'

Harker peered across at him through small round spectacles. The glass of one lens reflected the light intermittently, causing Angel to narrow his eyes from time to time.

'So the great almighty Inspector Angel is not as great and almighty as all that, then?' Harker said. 'All that stuff that you feed the newspapers and magazine journalists is just so much blether, then, is it? The parallel drawn by some smart-arse reporters with you and the Canadian Mounties is only so much more flannel. Huh. The man who always solves his murder cases can't solve two in a row. Well, well, well. What have you to say to that?'

Angel didn't know what to say. His face was red. There was a fire raging in his chest, but he knew it would not pay him to say what he thought. Eventually he answered in a controlled, even voice. 'I do the best I can,' he said. 'I expect to make an arrest for the murder of Ian Fairclough quite soon.'

Harker smiled.

It was very unusual, Angel remembered. It was said that every time Harker smiled a donkey died.

'Do you want me to pass the other case on to another detective?' Harker said.

Angel frowned. He couldn't think of who he might be thinking of. Inspector Asquith wasn't a detective, and besides, he had plenty to do. The uniformed division was a much bigger section than CID. He surely wasn't thinking of DS Crisp, DS Carter or DS Taylor? There was nobody else he could think of. He would have to reply very soon. And there was only one answer.

'No, sir,' he said. 'Of course not.'

'I was thinking, maybe a fresh face to the problems?' Harker said with a grin. He was enjoying the barracking.

'I don't think so, sir.'

'Well, Angel, I will have to do *something*. What do you suggest?'

Angel sighed. 'I still have some ideas of my own, sir,' he said. 'I have by no means exhausted my investigations.'

Harker shook his head, but he was still smiling. 'I think you have, lad. I think you've hit a brick wall. I've been too lenient with you. Let you have your head far too long. I may have to rein you in.'

Angel felt very much like a mouse being played with by a cat. He decided to call his bluff. 'Very well, sir,' he said. 'If you want me to relinquish the cases, I can do that.'

'Aaaaah!' he said, his eyes shining like searchlights. 'I *thought* you were beaten. I said all along that—'

Angel was furious. 'I am *not* beaten. Far from it. I expect to be able to solve both of these cases given the time and the opportunity. You seemed to want me to leave these cases, so I offered to get out. That's all.'

'You mean resign from the force?'

'Certainly *not*!'

Harker pursed his lips. 'Well, Angel, what *do* you mean? We seem to have reached an impasse.'

'There's no impasse,' Angel said. 'If you let me get on with it, I think I can solve those cases in a week or so, sir.'

'I suppose out of respect for the lifetime's service your father gave to the force and your service of twelve years, I could—'

Angel corrected him. 'Sixteen years.'

'Sixteen years, then, I could allow you a little leeway. I'll give you four days. I expect you to have solved the murders and charged somebody, approved by the CPS, by next Monday. Now I can't say fairer than that, can I?'

Angel's eyes shone. 'That's only *two* working days,' he said. 'I said a week.'

'That's the best I can do, Angel.'

THIRTEEN

Angel stormed his way down the corridor in the direction of the CID office. Ahmed was by the door seated at a computer. When he saw Angel, he jumped to his feet.

'Can I help you, sir?' Ahmed said.

'I am looking for Flora Carter.'

'I'll find her, sir. Or she might have gone out.'

Angel ran his hand through his hair. 'I hope not. I want her urgently.'

'Right, sir,' he said, and he rushed off.

Angel then made his way to his own office. He reached the desk and sat down. He took a sheet of Bromersley Police printed letterhead and wrote the following by hand.

To Professor A.P. Lott,
Wetherby Police Ballistics Laboratory.

Dear Professor,

Thank you for the confirmation that the Walther PPK/B.32 was definitely used to kill Joan Minter.

Regarding the Ian Fairclough case, I have now discovered the identity of the man previously described only as 'the big man in the black overcoat' and will be making an arrest in a dawn raid on Saturday morning.

It will mean working most of the weekend, but I am glad to say that Mary will not be put out by this as she is presently away visiting her sister and I have the house to myself. It is also a good excuse for me to dine out at The Feathers Hotel.

Best wishes,

Yours sincerely,

Michael Angel.

When he had finished he looked at it, nodded with satisfaction, reached out for an envelope and addressed it.

There was a knock at the door.

'Come in,' he said. It was DS Carter. 'You wanted me, sir?'

'Right on cue,' he said, and he handed her the handwritten letter. 'Read that, Flora,' he said.

She read it and looked at him with narrowed eyes and a crinkled brow.

He told her about the leak of information that was finding its way to the *Daily Yorkshireman.*

'And what do you propose to do with this letter, sir?' she said.

'I have not told anybody that my wife is away, Flora. At the moment, only *you* know. By tomorrow morning, I expect all of Yorkshire to know. But until then, keep it to yourself. This letter is part of a trap. I expect to catch two birds with one stone.'

Her eyebrows shot up and her mouth dropped open. 'How's that going to work, sir?'

'I'll tell you. I need your help.'

Angel's pulse rate increased as he explained how he knew that somebody in the police station was giving or selling inside information to the *Daily Yorkshireman*. He detailed the plan he had to catch the rogue and, at the same time, hopefully, the murderer of Ian Fairclough. He told her he had not discussed any of this with anybody else and insisted that she did not tell anyone of the plan.

She listened attentively and readily agreed to keep silent. She was delighted to be his confidante. She asked a couple of questions and was satisfied with the answers and so the plan was triggered into action.

Her eyes sparkled and she felt a lightness in the chest.

'You'd better push off, Flora,' he said. 'You've a few things to see to, and so have I. Send Ahmed in to me, will you?'

She smiled, nodded and said, 'Right, sir.'

She bounded out of the room and closed the door.

Angel folded the letter to the professor in Wetherby, put it in the addressed envelope and sealed it.

There was a knock at the door. 'Come in.' It was Ahmed.

'I've been through to Records, sir,' he said. 'And there were only four people who were known to wear rings depicting a skull or a skull and crossbones. Three of them are dead and the fourth is in custody in HMP Barlinnie — that's in Glasgow.'

Angel blew out a lungful of air and said, 'Thank you. And I know where Barlinnie is, lad.'

Ahmed smiled and turned to go.

'Just a minute,' Angel said.

Ahmed turned back.

'I have a very urgent and confidential message I want to go by courier today,' Angel said, handing him the envelope.

'Right, sir,' Ahmed said. He went out and closed the door.

Angel opened a desk drawer and looked around for his police telephone directory, then he took out his mobile and tapped in a number.

'Wetherby Police Ballistics Laboratory,' a voice said.

Angel said, 'I want to speak to Professor Lott, please.'

Angel arrived home at 5.30 p.m. that Thursday teatime. The house was quiet, cold and dark and there was no Mary to greet him. And no hot meal to look forward to.

He switched on the kitchen light, the central heating, then the radio in the kitchen. He went into the hall, took off his coat and tossed it onto the newel post. He noticed some post on the carpet and picked up two envelopes. One was from a firm called Cable and Light he had never heard of. They were offering an 'unbeatable broadband deal', it said on the envelope, and the other was from The International Regal Gold Insurance Company eager to insure his wheelchair, stairlift and caravan free of charge. There was no hurry to deal with either of them as he was committed to his present internet supplier for another nine months and he didn't have a wheelchair, stairlift or caravan. He put the circulars on the sideboard in the sitting room and returned to the kitchen. He opened the cupboard, took out a tumbler, then a beer from the fridge. He was about to pull the ring to open the beer when he stopped. He looked round the kitchen. He pursed his lips, creased his eyes for a few moments, then made a decision. He nodded and determinedly put the unopened can of beer back in the fridge and the tumbler back in the cupboard. He went back into the hall, dragged his coat off the newel post and put it on. He turned off the radio, opened the back door, turned out the light, went outside and locked the door.

Ten minutes later, he was walking into the dining room at The Feathers Hotel.

The following morning Angel called at a newsagent for a copy of the *Daily Yorkshireman* and in the BMW he quickly read their latest report on the investigation into the murder of Joan Minter. He smiled grimly when he saw that the bait in the trap had been taken. Also in the text it said that the Walther PPK/B.32 was used to kill Joan Minter, that Inspector Angel was planning to make an imminent arrest of the big man in the black coat and that he was able to devote all his attention to the case that weekend as his wife was away visiting family.

He nodded at all this with satisfaction. He closed the paper and drove to the police station.

As he made his way down the corridor, Flora caught up with him. She was carrying a copy of the *Daily Yorkshireman*. Her cheeks were flushed and her eyes shiny and bright.

'Good morning, sir,' she said. 'I see that the bait has been swallowed.'

He smiled. 'Yes, Flora,' he said. 'And the description of the gun, Walther PPK/B.32, was printed in the paper. Now, I wrote *that* in the letter as a deliberate mistake. There isn't such a weapon. It should have been Walther PPK/S.32.'

She had to step out quickly to keep up with him. 'We could make an arrest and get a conviction on the strength of that, sir,' she said.

'We could, but we won't. I want Ian Fairclough's killer before we do that.'

Angel had arrived at the door of his office.

'Come inside a minute, Flora,' he said.

He opened the door and went in. 'Sit down,' he said.

He took off his coat and sat down at the desk. He rubbed his chin thoughtfully.

'You know, I've been thinking,' he said. 'The murder of Joan Minter could very well have been somebody close to her.'

'Do you mean her ex-husbands, sir? Well, there *are* four of them.'

'No. I wasn't meaning close in that way, although we may have to go there if all else fails.'

'Do you mean the secretary or the butler?'

He nodded. 'They certainly had a better chance than anybody else, and they had the opportunity to plan it all so carefully.'

'Did you mean the secretary *and* the butler, sir?'

Angel's jaw dropped as he looked straight ahead and visualized the two people together. Then he looked at Flora and said, 'Maybe. Maybe. Alexander Trott has inherited Joan Minter's fortune, you know.'

Flora's eyes opened wide. 'That would be a big enough motive for some evil people. And I suppose they'd make a formidable team in their roles and in these circumstances.'

Angel wrinkled his nose. 'We need more information,' he said. 'The next closest people in this situation I suppose would be the caterers, the Joneses. You have their phone number and address. Give me the number,' he said, picking up the phone.

Flora dived into her pocket and took out her notebook. She flicked through the pages backwards, found it and read it out.

Angel tapped the number onto the pad and waited. He heard three electronic notes followed by a recorded voice that said, 'The number you have dialled has not been recognized. Please hang up and try again.'

Angel tried again and heard the same message.

He banged down the phone, then through clenched teeth said, 'That's not right, Flora. Sort it out. I want to see them ASAP.'

Her face tightened. Her eyes narrowed. 'I don't understand it, sir,' she said.

'Well, push off and come back when you've sorted it out. I want to speak to that chap Jones ASAP.'

She jerkily put up a hand to clear a few strands of hair away from her face as she made for the door.

Angel was trying to think what best to do next when the phone rang. He glared at it, then picked it up. It was a constable in the reception office.

'There's a lady here, sir,' he said, 'asking for you.'

'What does she want, lad?'

'She says she saw the photograph of the pickaxes in the *Chronicle* and that she sold three pickaxes to a man recently.'

Angel's face brightened. 'Bring her down to my office, will you.'

'Righto, sir,' he said.

Three minutes later, the constable showed a woman in her fifties into Angel's office. 'Mrs Pickles,' he said.

'Thank you, Constable,' Angel said.

'Right, sir,' he said, and he went out and closed the door.

'Please sit down, Mrs Pickles. Thank you for coming in.'

'Thank you, Inspector. I hope I can help.'

‘I understand that you sold three pickaxes to a man recently.’

‘Yes. Me and my husband have a shop at the other side of Tunistone,’ she said. ‘In the middle of nowhere, you might say. We sell everything — mostly to farmers. My husband has put a sign up on the end of the shop, what says, “If I haven’t got it, you don’t want it.”’ She laughed. ‘He’s a card is Denzil and no mistake.’

‘And you sold three pickaxes to a man recently?’ Angel said.

‘Yes. I’m coming to that, young man,’ she said. ‘Rush. Rush. Rush. Everybody’s in too much of a rush these days. There’s no time to enjoy yourselves.’ She looked round the office. ‘Do you know, I’ve never been in a police station before.’

Angel looked round the office with her. He had not looked round the place in the way Mrs Pickles was looking at it for years. He realized that perhaps it could do with a coat of paint. He looked back at her.

‘It was on Monday morning when a strange car pulled up outside the shop,’ she said.

‘Can you describe it?’ he said.

‘No need to. Tell by the rattle,’ Mrs Pickles said. ‘Well, it wasn’t any of the tractors I knew. It wasn’t a Land Rover, it wasn’t the vicar’s Ford, and it wasn’t Mrs Mackenzie, so it had to be somebody what I didn’t know.’

Angel’s eyebrows went up. ‘You didn’t see it, then?’

‘Haven’t time. Anyway there’s no need. Know them all by the sound they make.’

Angel frowned. ‘The sound?’ he said.

‘Yes. The rattle of the doors or the exhaust or the purr of the engine or whatever. Being a detective, you’ll know all about that.’

His eyebrows shot up. He tilted his head to one side as he pursed his lips.

‘Do you want to know about the man what came in?’ she said.

'Yes, please,' he said.

'Well, then, a big, lumpy, unhappy man comes in. He looks around . . . sees the display of Stronghold tools. Marches over to it. Picks up a pickaxe. Fingers the business end of it. Then he looks round and sees me. "Have you got three of these?" he says. I looks at him strangely. I mean, who would want *three* of them? Anyway, I think we have, I said. And I went in the back to where the rest of the stock is. I find him two more and takes them out to him.'

'Can you describe him?'

She screwed up her face and shook her head. 'Big. *Very* big. And ugly. *Definitely* ugly,' she said.

'Can you describe his features?'

'He didn't have any features. He was just plain ugly. I've seen things floating in vinegar look better. His mother should've asked for a refund.'

Angel didn't smile at the quip. He pursed his lips, then said, 'What colour was his hair?'

'Black. As black as the ace of spades.'

'And what was he wearing?'

'Well, he wasn't no farmer. I can tell you that. I could tell that from his boots. I always looks there first. You can tell a lot from what a man has on his feet. A farmer's boots are always mucky. This man's were clean.'

Angel nodded. 'What else?'

'A big black overcoat. That would have set him back a few quid. It would have to have been made to measure. That's all I noticed.'

Angel lowered his eyebrows. 'And what makes you say he was an "unhappy" man?'

'Well, he pushed his way into the shop and straightaway asked about the pickaxes. No "Good morning". No "How are you?" No "What a nice day it is". Nothing. He didn't have a word for the cat. He took the pickaxes, paid for them and went off. Again, no "Thank you". No nothing.'

Angel rubbed his chin. 'Perhaps he had a lot on his mind.'

'I've a lot on my mind, but I reckon I knows my p's and q's.'

Angel smiled. 'Do you think you'd recognize him if you saw him again?'

'Definitely. Absolutely. Oh yes, sir. I can say that without fear of contraception.'

He smiled.

FOURTEEN

There was a knock at the door.

'Come in,' Angel said.

It was Ahmed. 'You wanted me, sir?'

'Yes, lad. Just checking. Yesterday I gave you an important letter for urgent delivery.'

Ahmed frowned. 'Yes, sir. It was addressed to Professor Lott at Wetherby.'

'That's the one. What did you do with it?'

'I gave it to Mrs Meredew, the telephone receptionist, sir. And I told her it was urgent and that you wanted it sending by courier.'

Angel smiled. 'Did anybody else see it before you gave it to her?'

Thoroughly mystified, Ahmed said, 'It was sealed, sir.'

'I know that. *I* sealed it. I just want to be quite clear about it. You didn't open it or show it to anyone else?'

Ahmed opened his eyes in astonishment. 'Of course not, sir,' he said.

'I was sure you hadn't,' Angel said with a benevolent smile. Then he explained the trap that he had set to catch Mrs Meredew, and told him to keep the matter to himself.

'Right, sir,' Ahmed said, and he left Angel's office. He grinned at the deception and was delighted to be let in on the ruse. He didn't like Mrs Meredew anyway. She was always offhand with him. He thought that maybe she didn't like black people. He was still smiling when he reached his desk in the CID office.

Ten minutes later, Flora Carter arrived at Angel's office.

'The number that Jones the caterer gave me has never been an allocated phone number, sir,' she said. 'And the address he gave me is also false. There isn't a number 82 Eastgate. The numbers stop at 56.'

Angel's face creased. 'Right, Flora. Get me Jane Bell's telephone number. And the butler, Alexander Trott's.'

Two minutes later, he was speaking to Jane Bell.

'It's nothing to worry about, Jane. I have need to speak to Miss Minter's caterers, the Joneses. We are having a bit of difficulty contacting them. Do you have their latest telephone number and address?'

'I don't, Inspector, I'm very sorry. I didn't have anything at all to do with the catering arrangements for her party. She wanted to do as much of it as she could herself, you know.'

'Well, what do you know about the Jones couple, Jane?'

'Nothing really, Inspector. I showed them round when they came to see Miss Minter, that's all,' she said.

He frowned. 'Showed them round?' he said.

'They came by arrangement with Mr Trott, on Saturday, the day before the party. They wanted to see the kitchen facilities, the proximity of the drawing room to the kitchen, the positioning of the electric sockets and the switches. Things like that. They depend a lot on electric sockets for their pans and hotplates.'

'Of course. Why did Miss Minter choose the Joneses to cater for her special party?'

'I don't know. Mr Trott had probably heard of them. They may have been recommended to her by a friend. Or it may have been one of those decisions Miss Minter had made herself. I'm sorry, I can't help you with that one.'

'Were they at any time left in the big drawing room by themselves?'

Jane Bell hesitated. 'Yes. They were. I was busy with the delivery of wines and spirits from Heneberry's at the time. I had to leave them for a while . . . might have been twenty minutes or so.'

'Aaaah,' Angel said knowingly. He smiled, but it was a grim smile.

'But everything was all right,' she said quickly. 'I checked the rooms personally. Everything was left just as it should have been.'

'I'm sure it was, Jane,' Angel said, his eyes suddenly beginning to glaze over. 'I'm sure it was . . . thank you.'

He replaced the phone and, keeping his hand on the instrument, he smiled, then sighed deeply.

Flora saw the transformation in him and said, 'Do you want Mr Trott's phone number, sir?'

He didn't reply. She wasn't sure whether he had heard her or not.

'What did she say, sir?' she said.

Angel slowly looked at Flora, then shook his head to clear it and said, 'I think we might have Joan Minter's murderer.'

It was 6.30 p.m. that Friday evening.

The police station was so quiet you could have heard the sound of a tenner being slipped into a screw's pocket.

Angel was still at his desk. He phoned The Feathers Hotel and booked a table for dinner for himself that evening for 7 p.m. He cleared the desk of the reports he had read, then he opened a drawer in the desk and took out the Glock 17 handgun and the fully loaded magazine he had withdrawn from the armoury that afternoon. He pushed the magazine into the gun and put it into his jacket pocket. He then went out of the station to his car at the rear of the station. He drove the BMW out of the station car park into town to The

Feathers Hotel. He parked the car near the main door. He went into the bar and looked round. There were only six men in there. He clocked them. He didn't know any of them. He went up to the bar, ordered a whisky and asked for the restaurant menu. He took them away with him to a seat near the door. He wanted to see out of the corner of his eye if anybody was paying him any attention. He didn't think anyone was.

At 7 p.m. he went into the restaurant. He was the first there and had an unexceptional meal. At 7.50 p.m. he left The Feathers and went outside to his car. The sky was as black as an undertaker's hat.

He arrived home around 8 p.m. He drove straight into the garage, pulled down the door, locked it and looked around. It was as quiet as it was dark. He put his hand in his pocket as he walked down the garden path. The phone was ringing as he came through the door. It seemed to have an imperative sound to it. He switched on the light and quickly dashed over to it and snatched it up.

'Hello?' he said, but the line was dead.

It worried him. He didn't like calls that resulted in silence like that. He put down the receiver and went round the room closing the curtains.

Then he had an idea. He slumped down in the chair and tapped in 1471. Up came a number he recognized. It started 013: the Edinburgh prefix. Then he remembered. His wife's sister, Miriam, had had her operation that morning. He'd better ring back straight away and show some concern, although he was confident that she would be OK. She always was.

He picked up the phone and tapped in the number.

'Hello, sweetheart. How are you?' he said.

'Fine. Fine,' Mary said. 'Oh, I'm so relieved. I've been ringing all evening. I couldn't get you. Where have you been?'

'Working,' he said quickly. 'But I've been thinking of you. Tell me, how is Miriam?'

'She's fine,' she said. 'I am so relieved. She came out of the anaesthetic quite quickly. The surgeon's made a super job. He's ever so pleased with her, and she is with him. She has a lot of stitches, but he said they'd hardly be visible in a few weeks' time.'

Angel frowned. He wondered who would be looking at them anyway.

'And he's ever so nice,' she said. 'I've met him.'

'At what those cosmetic wallahs charge, he should be oozing charm from every orifice,' Angel said.

His comment rattled Mary. She didn't like him making critical statements. '*Michael!*' she snapped.

There was a brief silence.

'How are *you* getting along?' she said. 'What have you had for tea, love?'

'It was very nice, thank you,' he said quickly. 'When are you coming home?'

'Monday or Tuesday, if you can manage without me?'

'Of course I can manage without you. I don't want to have to, but I can. How are the kids behaving?'

'No problems at all. I take them to school for a quarter to nine and collect them at four o'clock. They're as good as gold. There's a steak and kidney pudding in the fridge — have you eaten it yet?'

'Yes. I think so. It was absolutely delicious.'

'What do you mean, "I think so"?'

He assumed the slightly-cross-husband tone. 'Look, Mary, this phone call is costing an arm and a leg. We shouldn't be using it to talk about food. I'm fine. The fridge is fine. Everything here is fine. Miriam's fine. The kids are fine. You're fine, and I'm looking forward to picking you up at the station on Sunday. In fact I can't wait.'

'Oh, darling,' she suddenly said gently. 'I *do* believe you're missing me. That's nice. I'm missing you too, but it can't be before Monday.'

'Yes, all right, sweetheart, Monday. Now, give my love to Miriam and the kids. And I'll give you another ring soon. God bless you.'

'And God bless you,' she said. 'Bye.'

He replaced the handset. And smiled. He loved Mary more than words could possibly quantify but he couldn't make love to her over the phone. He wanted her home and he was delighted to learn that she was returning on Monday. By then he should have solved the two murder cases and got the killers behind bars.

He took off his jacket, slumped down in his favourite chair and switched on the television. He watched the news, the weather, the local news and then some new quiz game. He knew some of the answers but wasn't following the rules of the game and he didn't know any of the so-called celebrity contestants. He switched the television off, then prepared his breakfast before going upstairs.

It was 2 a.m. Angel heard the noise of a creaking floorboard on the stairs. He knew it was the fourth from the top. That step had always creaked. Thirty seconds later there was the rustling of clothes and the sound of a forty-a-day man refilling his lungs with air.

Angel froze and maintained absolute silence by inhaling and exhaling long, steady breaths.

He saw the silhouette of a small man carrying a partly masked torch come through the open bedroom door. The man was creating looming shadows on the wall of the dressing table, then the bedside lamp, then the bedhead.

The man came further into the bedroom. Through the crack in the hinge of the wardrobe door, Angel also saw that he was carrying a gun with a thickened barrel. It sent a shiver down his spine.

The torch shone fully on the bed. It showed the shape of Angel's body under the duvet. The intruder raised his gun with the silencer on it and fired at the duvet three times. There were three quick thuds as lead hit the duvet. He then went back to the wall by the door to switch on the room light, stuffed the gun in his pocket and approached the bed. He pulled back the duvet to look at his handiwork and saw an arrangement of pillows and cushions. His eyes went cold. His face turned scarlet. '*What the hell?*' he said.

At that moment, Angel pushed open the wardrobe door behind him, shoved the muzzle of the Glock just above the man's coccyx and said, 'Throw the gun to the floor on the other side of the bed, then put up your hands, unless you want to spend the rest of your life in a wheelchair.'

The man stiffened. 'All right,' he said. 'You got me. Don't shoot.'

Angel jabbed the Glock harder into his back and through clenched teeth he said, '*Do it, then. Throw it.*'

'I'm doing it. I'm doing it,' the man whined.

He reached down to his pocket, took it out and threw it as instructed. Then he put up his open hands.

The gun landed on the carpet on the other side of the room.

'That's better,' Angel said. 'I wondered when you'd show up, Roberto.'

The man stiffened. '*What?*' he said.

'I have suspected you for some time,' Angel said. 'Roberto Fachinno, also known as Robert Jones, erstwhile caterer, son of Charles Fachinno, the potted-meat king. Turn round. I am arresting you for the murder of Joan Minter.'

Roberto Fachinno turned so that he had his back to the bed, while Angel faced him with his back to the bedroom door.

The man said, 'Go ahead. Arrest me. *Then* you'll have to prove it.'

'I will. And I can,' Angel said.

'Impossible. I am completely innocent,' Roberto Fachinno said.

'I know exactly how you murdered Joan Minter. It was really quite clever.'

'Ridiculous,' Roberto Fachinno said. 'Nobody will believe you.'

Angel said, 'Oh yes they will. You went to Joan Minter's home a few days before the big occasion purporting to sort out her requirements in detail, but you actually came to familiarize yourself with the switches on the panel by the drawing-room door. You had to know *that* to put your plan into action. Then, on Sunday night, when Miss Minter was addressing her guests, you sneaked out of the kitchen into the hall and when she had everybody's attention, you crept into the room, behind the guests, waited for her to put the cigarette to her lips, then switched off the lights, aimed for the cigarette and pulled the trigger. Then you rushed out into the hall, opened and closed the front door to make everyone think you had gone outside and then swiftly returned to the kitchen.'

'Ha!' Roberto Fachinno said. 'And why would I want to do all that to murder an old, forgotten film star?'

'Revenge. Revenge for the bankruptcy of your father. He always blamed Miss Minter for reneging on her commitment to take the lead in a film he was planning to make.'

'Very clever. I am glad that you know, Angel. I wish the whole world could be told that my father was an honourable man, and I am glad that you know even though you are so near the end of your life.'

Angel thought it was very bold of Roberto to imply that he had the upper hand.

'She not only reneged,' Roberto continued. '*She broadcast* the fact that she had reneged. She said that she couldn't consider taking on such a role for an unknown entity whose only claim to the entertainment industry was that he was "the potted-meat king". She had such influence. She seemed *so* respectable . . . *so* shrewd . . . *so* charming, that everybody else in the film-making business deserted him. My father couldn't attract actors of her standing to consider taking the role. It made him bankrupt. *My father*. A man who was always used to having a few hundred quid in his pocket was reduced to fishing for food through skips at the back of Cheapo's to survive.'

'*He* didn't murder anybody, though, did he?'

'No. He was too weak. But I have now put that right. I am strong, you see, Angel.'

Angel looked him in the eye and smiled. 'Not strong enough, Roberto. I am taking you down to the station, where you will be charged with murder.'

'Oh no, you're not,' Roberto said. 'My brother Tony will explain. Tell him, Tony.'

Angel heard a rustle of clothes behind him and felt the cold muzzle of a gun being jabbed into the back of his neck.

'Drop it, Angel,' the other man's voice said.

Angel's heart missed a beat. He could also feel the hot breath of the man on his neck and cheek.

Angel dropped the Glock pistol onto the floor.

'You didn't think I'd walk into an ambush as easily as that, did you, Angel?' Roberto Fachinno said.

Angel's pulse beat in his ear and was almost exploding.

The big man's face went red. He glared at his brother and said, 'You know my name's not Tony, you frigging berk. Not Tony. It's Antonio, *Antonio*. How many times do I have to tell you?'

Then Antonio Fachinno turned back to the policeman and said, 'Hey, Angel, turn around. I wanna see your face. I don't want to shoot you in the back.'

Angel turned round to see the man with the gun.

He was a big man. A huge man. He had big ears, a big nose, black hair and he was wearing a black overcoat. It fitted exactly the description of the man several witnesses had seen in connection with the murder of Ian Fairclough.

Angel knew that the two brothers were very dangerous men.

Roberto came across to his brother and through clenched teeth said, 'It took you long enough to get here.'

He looked at him and sneered. 'I'm here, aren't I?' he said.

Roberto's lips tightened. 'We've been here far too long,' he said. 'We'll have to take him with us. Tie his hands.'

Antonio glared at his brother and said, 'What with?'

'Anything. See what there is.'

They glanced round the room, then back at Angel.

Antonio, seeing nothing suitable, looked at his brother, shrugged and held out a hand.

Roberto quickly said, 'Keep your eye on him, you berk.'

'I am doing.'

'He could be dangerous. He's a copper and he's supposed to be smart.'

'Huh. He don't look so smart just now, does he?' Antonio said with a grin. 'And there's nothing to tie up his hands.'

'His *tie*, you berk. Use his tie,' Roberto said.

Antonio glared at him. 'Don't speak to me like that or I'll frigging belt you.'

Roberto simply glared back at him.

The big man went up to Angel and reached up to his tie. He couldn't manage to loosen it while holding the gun so he dropped the gun into his pocket and had another try. Angel promptly reached into the big man's pocket and without taking the gun out, turned it towards Antonio's ample stomach and jabbed it in so that he was sure to feel it. The man gasped.

'Tell your brother to drop his gun,' Angel said quietly.

'Drop your gun, Roberto,' he said. 'He's got me.'

'You idiot!' Roberto said. 'What do you mean?'

Antonio's eyes were almost bursting out of their sockets. '*Drop the frigging gun!*' he said.

Roberto dropped the gun to the floor.

Angel jabbed the gun hard into the big man and said, 'A bullet in the stomach probably wouldn't kill you, Tony, but it would be mighty uncomfortable for a few months, so be very careful what you do, particularly in the next few seconds.'

Antonio's eyes flashed. 'Why? Why?' he said, in a voice two octaves higher. 'What are you going to do?'

'Roberto,' Angel said. 'I could soon put a bullet in your brother's stomach. It would mix well with that pork pie and milk he took from the Faircloughs' fridge after he murdered Ian Fairclough, wouldn't it?'

Roberto said, 'That was nothing to do with me. That's something he had to sort out himself. It was him that picked up the wrong suitcase.'

Antonio said, 'Shut your mouth, Roberto. Don't think you'll get away with this, Angel, because you won't.'

Angel looked into his eyes and smiled. 'Oh yes,' he said. 'I think I will.' Then he looked at Roberto and said, 'Go towards the window and stay facing it.'

The man didn't move.

Antonio swallowed three times quickly, then said, 'For God's sake do as he tells you. He's a frigging cop. He'll do it. He only needs a frigging excuse.'

Roberto moved slowly further down the bedroom, then turned to face the window.

Then Angel looked towards the bed and said, 'Right, Flora. Come out now and collect those two guns off the floor. There's mine and Roberto's.'

Antonio Fachinno's body stiffened at the news that someone else was in the room. Angel felt the slight movement. He jabbed him hard in the stomach with the gun. 'I shouldn't get any bright ideas, Tony,' Angel said. 'Remember this is your gun, and I just don't know how sensitive the trigger is.'

The big man froze.

Flora Carter slid out from under the bed, where she had been hiding. She had already collected one gun and scurried around on the floor for the other. She found it and stood up holding both guns.

Although a beautiful woman, she looked remarkably businesslike, holding a handgun in each hand.

'Do not hesitate to shoot either or both of these men, Flora, if they as much as twitch. They are both murderers. They are no loss to society.'

Her jaw was fixed. Her eyes monitoring everything. 'You can depend on it, sir,' she said.

Angel jabbed Antonio in the stomach once more, then quickly withdrew the gun from the big man's pocket and gave him a slight push to put space between them. Then

Angel stepped quickly backward a few paces to put several feet between them. He then stood there pointing the gun at him.

'Right, Flora,' Angel said, 'give me the Glock.'

She passed it to him.

Then he stood the brothers with their hands up, next to each other, facing the window and said to Flora, 'Right, I've got them covered. Have you got the handcuffs?'

'Six pairs, sir,' she said.

'We'll need three for these two. Hurry up. Fasten his left hand to Antonio's right. Then his right to the radiator, and then his left to the other end of the radiator.'

Flora went behind the brothers and worked quickly, fixing the handcuffs and clipping them tight shut.

Antonio said, 'What's this, Angel? You're stretching us out like washing on a frigging line.'

'It's not for long,' Angel said.

'You can't frigging do this,' Antonio said. 'I know my rights.'

Angel wrinkled his nose. 'Write your MP,' he said.

He gave each of them a pat-down search and checked their handcuffs. He glanced round the room, then he turned to Flora. 'Take this,' he said, pushing the gun taken from Roberto into her hand, 'and bring those other handcuffs.'

Then they ran downstairs, through the house in the dark to the back door and went outside.

FIFTEEN

Angel and Flora were both flushed and energized with their success at securing the Fachinno brothers, but the round-up was not finished yet.

Angel was thankful there was no moon. They looked up and down the street. There were no streetlights either. They were looking for a car with one or two men in it. There were a few cars parked on the street so they ambled slowly like a couple walking home after a late-night party, surreptitiously peering into each parked car as they passed it.

After a while, Angel gritted his teeth and said, 'Where are they?'

'I wonder if the Fachinnos drove themselves here,' Flora said.

'I wouldn't have thought so,' Angel said. 'They wouldn't have known whether they would need a quick getaway or not.'

Flora nodded in agreement.

'Let's try the next street,' he said.

They turned round, speeded up their walk to the other end, then made two right turns and resumed their apparently leisurely gait. They had walked only a few yards when they saw a saloon car with its red rear lights illuminated. In addition, there was just enough light to see in silhouette two heads of men in the front seats in earnest conversation.

Angel and Flora slowed down.

Angel realized that they had parked their car outside the house directly back-to-back with his house, so that the Fachinnos had only to trespass through the gardens of one house to reach their getaway car, which was prudently positioned out of sight.

Flora felt a tug at her coat. Angel was pulling her coat sleeve to bring her ear close to his mouth. 'Looks like this is the car. Go round that side,' he said. 'I'll take on the driver on this side.'

He arrived at the driver's door first. He took out the Glock and put his other hand on the door handle to open it but it was locked.

'Police!' Angel said. 'Would you get out of the car, please?'

The young man in the driving seat saw him. His eyebrows shot up and his mouth dropped open. He reached forward to the ignition key.

Angel promptly bashed the door window with the muzzle of the gun. The glass shattered into a thousand pieces. He reached inside and pressed down the door handle, the door was released and he pulled it open.

The car engine roared into life.

'Switch it off,' Angel said. 'I am a police officer.'

The young man pushed down the gear lever.

The car jerked forward and then stalled.

Angel grabbed the young man's arm and tried to pull him out of the seat, but he couldn't move him. He saw that the man's hand was gripping the steering wheel. He banged his fingers with the gun. The young man yelled and released his grip, then Angel dragged him out of the car, hanging on to his arm with a grip of steel.

The young man's other arm and his legs were flailing about frantically, and a few punches and kicks were landing on Angel's face and shins.

Angel retained his grip on the man's arm. He pocketed the handgun, pulled him in close, grabbed his wrist, turned it round and pulled his hand up his back with a jerk.

The young man screamed.

The attack on Angel ceased.

The young man pulled a face. 'Hey! That frigging hurts,' he said.

Angel pulled round the other arm, then reached into his pocket for a pair of the handcuffs and snapped them onto his wrists. He noticed the young man was wearing a big silver ring on the middle finger of his right hand. He saw in the dim light that it represented a skull. He nodded grimly.

'What's your name, lad?' Angel said.

The young man struggled with the handcuffs and said, 'Hey! What's this for?'

'What's your name?'

The young man stopped struggling, looked straight ahead and said, 'No comment.'

That reply told Angel that he had been through police hands before. He rubbed his chin and, holding him only by the handcuffs, said, 'I am arresting you for the murder of Joan Minter and Ian Fairclough.'

'*What?*' I had nothing to do with *them*,' he said. 'I put my hands up to some things but not *murder*!'

'Well, I know that I can book you for being one of two men who stole a woman's handbag and subsequently two cars. So let's start with you giving me your name.'

'Not me. And I don't know anything about that. No comment.'

Angel wrinkled his nose. 'Is that going to be your reply to all my questions?'

There was a pause then he muttered, 'No comment.'

Angel shook his head. 'Very well, lad,' he said. 'If that's how you want it,' he added with a shrug.

He turned to see how Flora was progressing.

She had succeeded in opening the nearside car door and was trying to get the other young man out. He was younger and not as tall or heavy as Angel's prisoner.

'For the last time, will you get out of the car?' she said.

The young man glanced at Angel holding his associate by the cuffs. 'All right. All right,' he said. 'I'm coming.'

He slowly got out of the car, turned to face Flora and said, 'What's up? What do you want, darling? I fink you fancy me, don't you?'

Flora's face muscles tightened. 'Turn around. Put your arms behind your back and put your wrists together.'

'Chatting me up, are you?' he said. He turned round and looked back at her over his shoulder. 'Wanna go out wiv me, do yer?' he said. 'What's *your* name, darling?'

Flora wrinkled her nose. She sighed loudly. 'Put your wrists together.'

Angel heard all this. 'You'd better do as my sergeant says, lad,' he said, 'before she kicks it out of you.'

'Huh,' he said. 'And they say there's no police brutality.'

He slowly turned and put his hands behind his back.

She produced a pair of handcuffs and had them tight around his wrists quicker than a pickpocket can take a wallet.

'What is your name?' she said.

'Well, my friends call me David, but you can call me *Mr* David,' he said with a snigger.

'And what's your last name?'

'Beckham,' he said with another inane snigger.

'David Beckham,' she said. 'I'll book you in that name if you want to be seen as a real idiot.'

Angel said, 'Book him in that name for now, Sergeant. I have a feeling that we'll soon know his name when we've taken his fingerprints.'

'You're not taking my frigging fingerprints. What do you want to know for?' he said.

Flora said, 'You are under arrest for the murders of Joan Minter and Ian Fairclough.'

'What? No, not me. I might a done a bit of feefing, in my time. I might put my hand up to that, but not murder, no, not me.'

Angel took out his mobile and scrolled down to a number and clicked on it.

A voice said, 'Control Room, DS Clifton.'

'DI Angel, Bernie. All right, send the Black Maria *now*.'

'Immediately, sir. It is standing by. Everything go to plan, sir?'

'Perfectly, Bernie. Perfectly.'

It was 4.40 a.m. on Saturday morning, 8 November. In the cold stark lighting of the charge room, under the super -vision of DI Angel, the four men were processed one at a time by Sergeant Clifton and two PCs. They were photographed from the front and in profile, then fingerprinted; the contents of their pockets were taken and they exchanged their clothes for denims provided by the police. Their own clothes were separately bagged, labelled and taken down to the SOCO office for examination.

Angel's face brightened when a part pack of Adelaide cigarettes and a silver cigarette lighter were taken out of Antonio Fachinno's pocket. Angel had them transferred to a separate evidence bag, which he labelled himself, then stuffed into his pocket for his early attention. He also took temporary possession of the silver skull ring, which was on the getaway driver's finger.

Flora Carter took the gun that had been in the possession of Roberto Fachinno alias Robert Jones out of her handbag. It was an old Smith & Wesson with a crude 2¼-inch-diameter silencer screwed onto the barrel. She opened the gun, spun the magazine and shook out the three remaining bullets untouched into an evidence bag. She looked on the body of the gun for the registration number. It was below the barrel. Under the mark MADE IN USA was stamped a long maker's number. She recorded it in her notebook.

Then she put the gun into another bag, labelled both bags, sealed them and brought them into Angel's office.

Angel did the same thing with the gun taken from Antonio Fachinno, which was a Beretta, a much smaller weapon but just as deadly. He then took them to the duty sergeant, instructing him to send them by courier to Ballistics in Wetherby, with a request that they report on them urgently by phone. He needed a comparison of the impressions the handgun firing pins made on the spent shell cases in each instance in order to verify that the particular shell came from the particular gun. The Glock he returned to the station armoury complete with the full magazine of seventeen unspent rounds.

Meanwhile Flora Carter emailed the photographs and the prints of the four men to Records, requesting information. She then sent the make and registration number of the two recovered guns to Records, both emails calling for an early response.

Then she went into Angel's office.

'I've sent the emails,' she said.

Angel looked at his watch. It was 6 a.m. It was still pitch-black outside.

He yawned and said, 'I think we can a call it a day.'

'Call it a *night*, sir.'

He smiled, stood up, reached out for his coat. 'Day or night, it's a job well done, Flora. Thank you.'

They made for the door.

Angel awoke at 1.30 that Saturday afternoon. He had to look at the clock on the bedside table and his watch next to it to confirm the time. Then he remembered why he was still in bed at that curious time. He'd had five hours' sleep and although rested, he had the feeling he had run a marathon.

He sat on the edge of the bed, stared at the Anaglypta and scratched his chest.

Bright daylight was peeping around the curtains.

He suddenly turned round and checked the duvet cover. It had bullet holes in it. So had the duvet, the sheet, the cover and the mattress. They would have to be replaced with new before Mary returned. He stood up and scratched his head. He surveyed the room. Everything else seemed to be in order. He pushed back the curtains, letting full daylight into the room. He had a quick wash in the bathroom, put on his dressing gown, then went downstairs.

The house was eerily quiet. He suddenly realized how much he missed Mary.

He ambled into the kitchen, switched on the radio, took a beer out of the fridge, a glass out of the cupboard and looked round for the frying pan. He looked on the gas hob, inside the oven, on the pan stand, round the kitchen; he even opened the pantry to see if it was in there. He couldn't see it anywhere. He stood in the middle of the little room and scratched his head. Then he sighed, shrugged, pulled the ring on top of the can and poured out the beer. He ambled into the hall, picked up the telephone directory and the phone, went into the sitting room and sat down in his usual chair. He looked up a number, tapped it out on the key pad and had a sip of the beer while it rang.

It took a long time but it was eventually answered.

The call was to Cheapo's, the hypermarket. He ordered a mattress and a duvet, both for a double bed, and a pair of sheets because they were not sold singly. He paid for them with his credit card, and they agreed to deliver them the next day even though it was a Sunday.

He looked at the oven again. He knew they had a frying pan. He had recently seen Mary using it. He stood there with his hand on his chin and his head tilted trying to think of where he had seen her put it. He didn't like to be beaten. But it was no good. He couldn't recall anything helpful.

He went over to the fridge and opened the door. It was bulging with food. He could see tomatoes, lettuce, celery, milk, margarine and so on. He wrinkled his nose and closed the door. He leaned down and pulled on the freezer door. Then he opened the top drawer. He picked up the nearest frozen lump. It said: 'Chicken breast. Thaw for twenty-four hours before cooking.' He threw it back in and fished around the rock-solid blocks of food. His eyes alighted on a pack of sausages. His eyebrows shot up. He picked it out and read Mary's label. 'Thaw for twenty-four hours before cooking.' He pursed his lips, dropped it back in the drawer, pushed it shut, then closed the freezer door.

He looked at his watch. It said ten minutes to two. He made a decision. He finished off the beer, pushed the can into the waste bin, rinsed the glass and left it to drain on the draining board. Then he dashed upstairs, shaved and dressed and came down as smart as paint.

He was at the door of the restaurant at The Feathers at five minutes past two. But he couldn't open it. He thought it might be stiff, but it wasn't. The door was locked.

He went into the bar. A barman came over to him.

'Is the restaurant not open?' Angel said.

'It *was*, sir. It closed at two.'

Angel clenched his fists.

'We can do you a snack in here, sir,' the barman said, reaching for a menu.

'Er, right. No, thank you,' Angel said.

He came out of the bar. He sighed noisily. Then he dashed out to the car and pointed the bonnet of the BMW to his home. He was annoyed that he was having so much difficulty just to feed himself. He had driven about a mile when he remembered that up a side street in the middle of an estate was a small frontage of five or six small shops. One of those shops was a fish and chip shop. He turned off there and found the place. It was open. And there wasn't a queue. He leaped out of the car and bounded up to the counter.

'Cod and chips, please,' he said to the man with the scoop.

'No cod,' the man said. 'It's haddock, is that all right?'

'Absolutely,' Angel said, his face glowing.

The man doled out a generous portion of chips, pulled a fish on top of them, wrapped them tightly and placed them on the counter.

Angel smiled, paid him and came out of the shop.

Angel had had a quiet Sunday, apart from the delivery of the new mattress, sheet, duvet and duvet cover, which he duly assembled on the bed. The pattern of the duvet cover was a similar floral pattern and he hoped that Mary wouldn't notice until he'd been able to give his whitewashed account of what had happened in the house while she had been away. He would only mention it if she spotted the difference.

It was 8.28 a.m. on Monday, 10 November when he made his way down the station corridor to his office where he took off his coat and hat and sat down at his desk. He reached out for the phone and tapped in the number of the CPS and made an urgent appointment to see Mr Twelvetrees at 2 p.m.

Then he phoned the CID office.

Ahmed answered.

'I want you to find DS Crisp and DC Scrivens and send them to my office ASAP.'

'Right, sir,' Ahmed said.

Angel replaced the phone. It immediately began to ring. It was the superintendent.

'Angel?' Harker said. 'You're always on the bloody phone when I want to reach you.'

Angel pulled a face. 'It was only an internal call, sir,' he said.

'I haven't time for complex explanations, lad. Bring yourself up here, *smartly*!'

'Right, sir,' he said, but the phone was already dead.

Angel's muscles tightened. He really detested meetings with the superintendent. His daily reports managed to avoid face-to-face contact much of the time. But Harker was his boss and contact was inevitable.

Angel trudged up to his office. He really did have some very good news to report. He had solved at least one of the murders and had the men responsible locked up.

He knocked on the superintendent's door.

'Come in,' Harker called.

The room reeked of menthol and the superintendent's desk was the usual chaotic mess.

Harker looked over the piles of papers, files and medications and said, 'You needn't sit down, Angel. You're not stopping long.'

Angel wasn't unhappy about *that*.

'When I came in this morning, I saw that four of the cells were occupied,' Harker said. '*Four!*' he bawled. 'In addition, I discovered that they had been in use since early on Saturday morning. We can't be catering for four villains for days on end like this. What do you think this is? The Dorchester? It ties up a man running after them and it costs hard cash to feed them, and that all comes out of our general account, which is sadly in the red again for this fiscal year. Have you got good, solid cases against all four?'

'I have a rock-solid case against all four for armed robbery of the Slater Security van, sir. I also have a rock-solid case against one of them for the murder of the actress, Joan Minter. And I expect to have enough evidence soon to make a case against another of them for the murder of Ian Fairclough.'

'If they are rock-solid cases, why have the villains not been charged?'

'We haven't had the time, sir.'

The skinny man's eyes almost popped out of his head. '*Time?* It only takes a few seconds to tell a man he is being charged with murder.'

'We didn't get away from here until after six o'clock on Saturday morning, sir.'

'If you really have solid cases against them, then they can be booted out of here and put on remand. They can eat and be looked after out of a prison's budget. Have you seen the CPS?'

'I have an appointment to see Mr Twelvetrees later today.'

Harker wasn't pleased. He pinched the bridge of his nose and squeezed his eyes tight shut. 'You'll miss the magistrates' court this morning, then?' he said.

The answer was obvious. Angel breathed in and out heavily. He didn't reply.

'Well, make sure they attend court tomorrow morning,' Harker said.

'I'll try,' Angel said. 'But they haven't seen their solicitors yet, sir.'

'Excuses. Excuses. That's all I get from you. I said make sure that they attend court tomorrow morning, and that's an order.'

'I'll do what I can, sir. There's something else I have to report.'

Harker's fists tightened. 'What is it?' he said.

'The woman in the reception office, Mrs Meredew, has been opening sealed communications that have passed through her hands and reported the contents to the newspaper, the *Daily Yorkshireman*.'

Harker's jaw dropped. He screwed up his face and scratched his left ear.

'Are you sure of that?'

'Positive. I made a simple, deliberate mistake in a letter sent to the lab at Wetherby by courier. The error was repeated the following day verbatim in the paper.'

Harker said, 'Mmmm. That explains a few things. She gave her notice in a week ago. I interviewed her to discover the reason. She simply said she was retiring. Mmmm. Anyway, there is a new woman starting today. But you should not be wasting your time checking out members of staff, Angel. That's not in your brief. *I* give you the cases you are to work on. You don't simply *assume* them.'

Angel's face reddened. His heart pounded like a steam hammer. 'What was I supposed to do, sir?' he said. 'Allow the leak to continue? She was giving away vital information that might have hindered the investigation.'

'You should have reported it to me. If I had decided there was anything in it, I would have instigated an inquiry. Instead you took on the job of investigating officer and now that she has left, it is rather too late. Any action I took against her would be pounced on by the media. And we don't want *that* sort of publicity. Would make it look as if we are unable to keep our own house in order. Anyway, as it happens she has already left, and, indeed, been replaced, so I am not disposed to take any action against her.'

SIXTEEN

Angel stormed out of Harker's office. He had a face like thunder. He marched down the green corridor to his own office where DC Scrivens and Ahmed were waiting for him.

He looked at Ahmed and said, 'Where's Crisp?'

'I told him you wanted to see him straightaway, sir,' Ahmed said. 'He said he would be here.'

Angel gritted his teeth, 'Right, lad,' he said. 'I need DS Carter as well. Ask her to come here ASAP.'

'Right, sir,' Ahmed said.

'And you'd better come back. There's a lot to do.'

Ahmed grinned. 'Right, sir,' he said as he went out.

Angel turned to Scrivens. 'Ted,' he said, 'the super wants those men out of our cells and put on remand post-haste. Will you find out who their solicitors are and arrange meetings ASAP? He wants me to arrange for them to appear before the magistrates tomorrow.'

'Tomorrow? That's a tall order, sir,' he said.

'Don't tell me, lad, tell the super.'

'I won't bother, sir,' he said with a knowing smile.

The look from him lightened Angel's mood and he smiled back.

He went out as Crisp came in.

'You wanted me, sir?'

Angel looked at him, then raised his eyes skywards, then shook his head.

Crisp said, 'I couldn't come sooner, sir. I had a member of the public who wanted to know—'

Angel put up both hands and blew out a length of breath. 'Don't bother, lad. Don't bother. I haven't the time or the patience.'

There was a knock at the door.

Angel turned to look at it and said, 'Come in.'

It was Ahmed. 'DS Carter's on her way, sir,' he said.

Angel nodded.

'And you wanted me to come back, sir?'

'Yes, Ahmed. Come in. Close the door. Wait a minute while I finish with DS Crisp.'

Ahmed nodded.

Angel turned back to Crisp. 'Right, now listen up. This is very important. I want you to go down to SOCO and see Don Taylor. He has a load of clothes and personal effects from the men in the cells. Among them is a large black overcoat. Ask Don to deal with it quickly, then let you have it and take it up to Dr Mac at the mortuary.'

'Right, sir,' Crisp said, and he turned towards the door.

'Just a minute,' Angel called. He quickly swivelled the chair through 180 degrees to the table behind him, picked up a small polythene evidence bag, turned back and handed it over to Crisp. 'In there is a very valuable button and some threads of cotton. You can see the threads hanging off the button without opening the bag, can't you?'

'Yes, sir.'

'A man's future hangs on what forensic science tells us about that button and those threads. Give that bag to Dr Mac also. He'll be expecting you. This is very, very important — and urgent.'

Crisp nodded and went out.

Angel then turned to Ahmed and said, 'Right, lad. Now what I have for you is equally urgent. Sit down a minute.'

Ahmed's eyes glowed with enthusiasm. He leaned forward. 'Yes, sir,' he said. He enjoyed being a policeman when he was busy doing something other than filing.

Angel took three other polythene evidence bags from the table behind him and passed them over to the young detective. 'There are three items taken from the gang we are holding in the cells,' he said. 'In one bag is a silver ring representing a skull, in another, a part pack of cigarettes and a lighter and in the third, a cigarette end with the brand clearly visible through the polythene. Take those to Mrs Sellars at 24 Ceresford Road. Ask the duty sergeant in the Control Room for some transport there and back. Tell him I have sent you and that it's urgent and important. Give Mrs Sellars my compliments and ask her if that is the skull ring she saw being worn by the man who knocked on her door on Monday last, 3 November. Then ask her if the cigarettes and lighter are hers and were the same ones in her handbag when it was stolen from her kitchen. And lastly, ask her if she could say that that cigarette butt could have been from a cigarette from the pack stolen from her. All right? Any questions?'

'Yes, sir,' he said. 'Do you want me to take a formal statement from her?'

'It would save time, yes, but let me know what her answers are on my mobile as soon as you can.'

'Right, sir.'

'There's something else,' Angel said. 'You must interview her without her husband being present. He doesn't approve of her smoking. If you ask about the cigarettes and the lighter in front of him, you'll make it very difficult for her. Understand?'

Ahmed smiled. 'Right, sir,' he said. Then he picked up the three evidence bags and went out.

Angel then reached out for the phone, scrolled down to 'Mortuary' and clicked on it. It was answered by Dr Mac. Angel told him that he was sending Crisp with the overcoat and button and asked him to treat the query with the utmost urgency. He asked him to report on the matter as soon as possible and certainly before Angel's meeting that afternoon with Twelvetrees at the CPS. Mac said he would do the best he could.

There was a knock at the door.

Angel finished the call to Dr Mac, then called out, 'Come in.'

DC Scrivens came in followed closely behind by DS Carter. She was carrying several A4 sheets of paper.

Angel looked at both of them and then back at Scrivens and said, 'Is it a quickie, Ted?'

'Yes, sir,' he said, looking deferentially at DS Carter.

She held out a hand, indicating that he should proceed before her.

Scrivens said, 'Well, sir, just to say that the solicitors of each of the four men say they will be round to see their clients before lunch.'

Angel sighed. 'Ah. Great stuff, Ted. Thank you.'

Scrivens nodded and went out.

Angel looked up at Carter and said, 'Now, Flora, what is it?'

She waved the papers she was holding. 'There's an email from Records, sir,' she said, sliding the sheets in front of him. 'It's the report on the two guns I asked them for.'

Angel picked it up eagerly. 'Ah yes,' he said. 'Sit down, Flora.'

He glanced at the brief accompanying letter then read the reports.

They said:

87 Beretta Cheetah 22LR/Wood Grip871FS SP677767765

Made in Italy by Fabrica d'Armi P Beretta. Distributed by Beretta USA Corp.

August 1982. Stolen in transit to retail gun shop in Smithville, Arkansas, USA.

14 April 2000. Found in raid on lock-up garage in London SW19 rented to Alan Patrick Elphinstone tried and acquitted of Hatton

Garden jewel robbery in June 2000. Gun could not be directly attributed to him.
28 August 2000. Delivered to RASC Cardiff for secure storage.
2 February 2001. Stolen from RASC Cardiff with other weapons. Present location unknown.

Smith & Wesson 38 Special CTG. Number 712530998
June 1941, one of an order for 180 from Smith & Wesson, Springfield, Massachusetts for US Marines, Com. Sit. 414. Lost in service in Hawaii USA between December 1950 and February 1951.
8 January 2000. Found in the possession of Leroy Nathan Carmichael by Glasgow Police, UK. Carmichael sentenced in Edinburgh to life imprisonment for murder of Elizabeth Naomi Carmichael and Anne Louise Carmichael.
1 September 2000. Delivered to RASC Cardiff for secure storage.
2 February 2001. Stolen from RASC Cardiff with other weapons. Present location unknown.

When Angel had finished reading the reports, he eagerly looked through the pile of papers on his desk. The pile was thick. There was a lot to go through but he knew exactly what he was looking for: it was another email with the history of the Walther handgun that Records had supplied a few days earlier. He found it and pulled it out. He quickly reread it. Then he smiled, looked up at Flora and said, 'All three guns were stolen from the army security store in Cardiff on 2 February 2001. As the Smith & Wesson and the Beretta were found in the possession of the Fachinno brothers, it is not surprising to find the third gun, the Walther, also in their hands, is it?'

'No, sir. It is not,' she said.

'Therefore if Dr Mac can forensically show that the button found in Ian Fairclough's hand irrefutably came from Antonio Fachinno's overcoat, with all the other witnesses' evidence and CCTV verification, and ballistic evidence that the Beretta taken from Antonio was the gun used to kill Ian Fairclough, we have a strong enough case to convince a jury that he murdered Fairclough to protect his identity while he was in the process of taking back the suitcase, which contained the proceeds from the raid on the Slater Security van.'

Flora frowned. 'How had Ian Fairclough come by Antonio Fachinno's suitcase, sir?' she said.

'His brother let it out. In my bedroom — you were under the bed. Antonio and Ian Fairclough had identical suitcases — brown and cream, very unusual — and they were both travelling on the same train to London. They must have been switched by accident at the ticket office or on the platform or on the train or in the buffet car. But let me continue . . . I don't want to lose my train of thought.'

'Right, sir.'

'Well, now, the gun — the Walther — that was found on the lawn at the home of Joan Minter was indeed the weapon used to murder her. We now know that for a fact. Also we know that Roberto was there. He was the caterer. He had motive, means and opportunity, and now we have shown that he had actual access to the Walther. Therefore, I am certain that a jury would convict him of that murder.'

Angel stopped. Looked at Flora and said, 'Have I forgotten anything?'

'Don't think so, sir.'

'Good. Well, then, leave me to it. I must get it written down for Twelvetrees while it is clear in my head.'

It was four o'clock when Angel came out of Twelvetrees' office. His face glowed. It shone as if it had been buffed up by a French polisher. He didn't walk, he glided his way along the pavement to the police station two buildings away. He sprang up the front steps, two at a time, then through the front door and the security door and made his way along the corridor towards his office.

DS Carter had been on the lookout for him. She had an urgent message to deliver. They met at the office door.

'Yes, Flora,' he said. 'Come in. What is it?'

She was smiling and holding several A4 sheets of paper. 'Got an email from Records, sir,' she said. 'A response to the photographs and prints I emailed there on Saturday. They have no knowledge of the Fachinno brothers. Their prints are not on record anywhere. But they know a lot about the other two: proper little heathens. List of offences — some on their own, some with each other. And they both have a list of offences for stealing expensive cars.'

'Have they been through our hands?'

'No, sir. But they're well known to Huddersfield CID.'

Angel nodded. 'That's great, Flora. Leave it all there,' he said, pointing to the corner of his desk. I'll read it when I've got a minute.'

She put the papers down and said, 'How did you get on with the CPS, sir?'

He leaned back in the chair, and formed a steeple with his hands. 'Everything is fine. We've got a prima facie case for both murders and the armed robbery provided that that button can definitely be proved to have come from Antonio Fachinno's coat, and that Ballistics confirm that the shells actually came from the two guns used to commit the murders.'

'That's good, sir,' she said.

'Now then, Flora, I've got another job for you,' he said. 'Now that we have photographs of the Fachinno brothers, I want you to include them in our rogues' gallery and take the laptop out to Mrs Pickles' shop on the High Street in Tunistone. She sold Antonio Fachinno the three pickaxes used in the robbery of the security van. I want her to pick him out. If she does — and I expect she will — take a statement from her. All right?'

'Right, sir,' she said. She went out and closed the door.

Angel rubbed his chin, then smiled. He liked it when the plan all came together.

The phone rang out.

It was Ahmed.

'Yes, Ahmed. What have you got?' Angel said.

'Mrs Sellars said that the lighter and cigarettes are hers, sir, that the cigarette end was almost certainly from the pack from her handbag because Adelaide cigarettes are not on sale over here, and that the silver ring certainly looks like the ring worn by the villain at her front door.'

Angel beamed. 'Right, lad, that's what I needed to hear. Now get it down on a witness's statement form.'

'Righto, sir.'

'Good. When you get back, bring it into my office. I've another job for you.'

'Right, sir.'

He ended the call and then looked at his notes. He didn't want to overlook anything. He still wanted to hear from Ballistics that the guns and shell cases matched; also he needed to know that *that* button came off Antonio Fachinno's coat.

Angel rubbed his chin and looked at the clock on the wall. It was five o'clock. It had been a great day.

On his way out of the station, Angel was thinking that it would be the last evening he would be dining alone. The following day, Mary would be home. It couldn't come soon enough. He felt a warm glow in his chest. He was meeting her at 5.35 p.m. at Bromersley Station. He began to think about what needed to be done to return everything to (what Mary would consider was) normal. He decided to defrost something from the freezer and make sure the house was tidy, warm and welcoming. He would get her some flowers, and he would wash up the few pots he had used, clean the sink, vacuum the carpets and maybe dust around. He thought that would about do it. He hoped that she wouldn't notice anything different about the mattress and the duvet. He hadn't yet thought of an explanation that would be acceptable to her for the fact that he had renewed most of the bedding.

After a couple of drinks in the bar at The Feathers and a steak and a half-bottle of house red in the restaurant, he called at the petrol station for some flowers, returned home and did the necessary chores. He phoned Mary in Edinburgh and confirmed the arrangements for meeting her the following day. Then he went to bed, and slept the sleep of the good.

It was 8.28 a.m. when he arrived back at his office the following morning, Tuesday, 11 November.

From his notes, he began to write out a preliminary list of charges against each of the four men who were to be presented in the magistrates' court later that morning. The list needed to be delivered urgently to the solicitor of the CPS, so when he had completed it, he summoned Ahmed and sent him round to their offices with it.

At 10.45 a.m., the Black Maria was backed up to the rear door of the station and the four men, each handcuffed to a PC, were led into the back of the vehicle for the very short ride two doors away to the court.

Angel walked round to the court. The preliminary hearing was expected to be at 11 a.m. prompt, but it was a few minutes late. As expected, the senior magistrate decreed that it was too serious a case to be heard there, and it would therefore be transferred to the Crown Court. Bail was requested but refused and the defendants were remanded to prison while the CPS and the defence teams prepared their cases.

At twelve noon, Angel returned to his office and was taking off his coat and hat when the phone rang out.

He quickly picked it up and sat down. It was Flora Carter.

'I'm outside Mr and Mrs Pickles' shop, sir, in Tunistone. Mrs Pickles looked through our rogues' gallery and immediately picked out Antonio Fachinno as the man who bought three pickaxes from her a week last Monday.'

Angel smiled. 'Great stuff, Flora. That will help to bottle them up for the security-van robbery.'

He ended the call and replaced the phone.

He glanced up at the clock. His eyes narrowed. He was anxious to hear from Mac. He hoped and prayed that the doctor would confirm that the button found in Ian Fairclough's hand was indeed originally from Antonio Fachinno's overcoat. He thought that Mac had had plenty of time to make the comparison. He was still reflecting about that when there was a knock at the door.

'Come in,' he called.

It was Ahmed. He was carrying a sheet of A4 paper. He handed it to Angel.

'Email from Ballistics, sir,' he said. 'The firing-pin marks on the spent shell cases perfectly match in both instances the examples fired in the laboratory.'

Angel sighed. 'Good. Great stuff,' he said, hardly giving the email a glance.

It was at that point the phone rang again.

Angel snatched it up.

His face brightened. 'Oh, it's you, Mac,' he said. 'I thought you had forgotten. I've been waiting for you to phone.'

'Well, I am here phoning you now,' the doctor said. 'I've had some analytical processes to go through. It all takes time. I wanted to be incontrovertibly certain that both the button *and* the cotton thread found in the victim's hand had come from Antonio Fachinno's overcoat.'

'And had they?' Angel said.

'Aye, they had.'

Angel closed his eyes. He said nothing for a second or two. Then he said, 'Thank you very much, Mac.'

SEVENTEEN

There was a cool wind blowing and the sky was dark when the 5.35 p.m. connecting train from Doncaster pulled into the station.

Angel was on the platform checking each carriage door as it passed him, looking for Mary's smiling face. At last he saw her. His heart warmed. He smiled and rushed towards her. She hadn't seen him. She was looking round. He followed the train and arrived at the carriage door at the same time the train stopped. She saw him then and both their smiles grew wider. He lifted her off the train, squeezed her, gave her a kiss, then leaned back into the doorway of the train to pick up her suitcase.

'Oh, darling,' Angel said. 'It's good to see you. Did you have a good trip?'

Mary tucked her arm into his and they walked along the platform. 'Very good, sweetheart. Have you been all right?'

He smiled and said, 'No. The house has been like a morgue. How is Miriam?'

'She's fine. The op did her good, I think. The doctor and the nurses pampered her and I think being on her own with the kids for so long, the time away from them has done her the world of good.'

He nodded. 'Are the kids all right?'

'I think they enjoyed the separation — although it was short — and they wanted it to last longer, but they weren't a bit of trouble.'

'Great,' he said. 'The car is parked in the little car park just up this rise.'

'Everything all right at work?' she said. 'The super keeping his distance?'

'Everything's fine. Just arrested the murderers of Joan Minter and Ian Fairclough.'

'Been busy, then?'

'Haven't had *you* bothering me,' he said with a smile.

'I'll have to go away again . . . for longer, a month or two . . . and much farther away.'

'You dare!' he said.

Mary laughed.

They reached the BMW.

Ten minutes later, they were home. Once inside they kissed again. Then Angel helped her prepare a meal. She looked into the freezer and found it almost as full as she had left it. She wasn't pleased.

'You've been eating out, haven't you,' she said.

'Only one night, I think,' he said. Then he said, 'Everything needed thawing out.'

'There was some salad. It was all prepared. You haven't touched it. Loads of tinned things you could have had. They didn't need thawing out.'

He looked down and ran three fingers across his forehead. 'I've been all right,' he said. 'By the way, where did you *hide* the frying pan?'

'I didn't hide it. It's kept with all the other pans,' she said, bending down in front of the oven. 'In this drawer.'

She pulled out a drawer that was below the actual oven, and sure enough, it was bursting with pans of all sizes.

'I didn't know it was a drawer. You never told me.'

She looked at him and narrowed her eyes. 'Besides, what did you want a frying pan for? You know I don't give you fry-ups. Anyway, Michael, you should have planned ahead. And taken the food out of the freezer a day or two before you wanted it.'

'I know. I know. I got that out, didn't I?' he said, pointing at the joint cooking in the oven.

'You did, darling, and it's *great* to be home,' she said.

He beamed.

They had their meal and she talked a lot about Miriam and the two children, about Edinburgh and how cold it had been up there.

Angel watched the late news on television while Mary cleared away and prepared breakfast, and they went to bed.

Mary didn't say anything about the mattress, the duvet or the duvet cover. Angel could hardly believe that she hadn't noticed. They cuddled up close together and he felt very guilty about the deceit of not telling her about the intruders and the gunshots but it would have made her extremely nervous.

'Isn't this bed wonderful?' she said. 'I'm afraid the bed I had at Miriam's was like rocks, but this is so comfortable. Do you know, Michael, I never appreciated just how really luxurious this bed feels? Aren't we lucky?'

In the darkness, Angel bit his bottom lip. He was uncomfortable at this less-than-ideal situation, but he could not tell her the truth. He was positive he was doing the right thing.

They fell asleep in each other's arms and woke up at the sound of the alarm at 7.30 the following morning.

Angel sat on the edge of the bed, scratched his head and shivered. He could feel Mary shuffling behind him. It's cold,' he said. 'Good morning, darling.'

'Good morning, sweetheart,' she said. 'It's to be expected. Winter is only round the corner.'

He shuffled into the bathroom and went up to the sink. He opened the cupboard over the sink and took out his razor, shaving brush and tube of shaving cream and began his ritual ablutions.

He heard Mary pass the open door on her way downstairs to prepare breakfast.

After a couple of minutes or so, Angel, all lathered up for a shave, shouted downstairs, 'Mary, there's no hot water.'

'Run the tap for a while,' she said.

'I have run it. I've run it for ages. What's happened? Have you run it all off or something?'

'No. I don't know. It's switched on. Looks like the boiler has packed in.'

'Can't have. Is it switched on?' he called as he leaned over to check the radiator in the bathroom.

'Of course it's switched on,' Mary said.

'This radiator is stone cold. The heating must be off too.'

'What did you do about that letter from the gas board?' Mary said. 'The one telling you that if we didn't replace the boiler soon, it might break down and they probably wouldn't be able to get the part.'

Angel's jaw dropped. He scratched his head. He frowned. He didn't know what to reply. Then he said, 'What did you say, love?'

THE END

ALSO BY ROGER SILVERWOOD

YORKSHIRE MURDER MYSTERIES

Book 1: THE MISSING NURSE
Book 2: THE MISSING WIFE
Book 3: THE MAN IN THE PINK SUIT
Book 4: THE MORALS OF A MURDERER
Book 5: THE AUCTION MURDERS
Book 6: THE MISSING KILLER
Book 7: THE UMBRELLA MURDERS
Book 8: THE MISSING MILLIONAIRE
Book 9: THE MISSING THIEF
Book 10: FIND THE LADY
Book 11: THE MISSING MODEL
Book 12: MURDER IN BARE FEET
Book 13: THE MISSING HUSBAND
Book 14: THE CUCKOO CLOCK MURDERS
Book 15: SHRINE TO MURDER
Book 16: THE SNUFFBOX MURDERS
Book 17: THE DOG COLLAR MURDERS
Book 18: THE CHESHIRE CAT MURDERS
Book 19: THE DIAMOND ROSARY MURDERS
Book 20: THIRTEEN STEPS TO MURDER
Book 21: THE FRUIT GUM MURDERS
Book 22: THE MONEY TREE MURDERS
Book 23: ANGEL AND THE ACTRESS

FREE KINDLE BOOKS

Do you love mysteries, historical fiction and romance? Join thousands of readers enjoying great books through our mailing list. You'll get new releases and great deals every week from one of the UK's leading independent publishers.

Join today, and you'll get your first bargain book this month!

www.joffebooks.com/contact

Follow us on Facebook, Twitter and Instagram

@joffebooks

Thank you for reading this book.

If you enjoyed it please leave feedback on Amazon or Goodreads, and if there is anything we missed or you have a question about, then please get in touch. The author and publishing team appreciate your feedback and time reading this book.

We're very grateful to eagle-eyed readers who take the time to contact us. Please send any errors you find to corrections@joffebooks.com. We'll get them fixed ASAP.

Printed in Great Britain
by Amazon

60152917R00111